I0822295

Not From Earth

Not From Earth Series
Book 1

Robert Adamson

Not From Earth

Book 1

by
Robert Adamson
www.robertgadamson.com

Epigraph

“The feeling is constantly growing on me that I had been the first to hear the greeting of one planet to another.”

– Nikola Tesla

Science Fiction

ISBN: 979-8-9864533-5-4 (Hardback)
ISBN: 979-8-9864533-6-1 (Paperback)
ISBN: 979-8-9864533-7-8 (Ebook)
ISBN: 979-8-9864533-8-5 (Audio)

U.S. Trademark SN 90760401:
NOT FROM EARTH

This book is for my family

Poetry by Dorothy Adamson, my mother

Prologue

The Ripley family's 1946 Hudson Commodore rolled south on Highway 285 toward Roswell, New Mexico. The two daughters, Joyce and Judee, held their spotted English Pointer, Bozo, across their laps and begged their mother again, "How much longer?"

Fifteen minutes later, their father, Charles Ripley, pulled the smooth-riding heavy green Sedan into a Chevron gas station. A well-groomed young man in a buttoned-up white shirt and a black bowtie came dashing out to assist. While the eager lad filled the tank, washed the windows, and checked the tires, Charles purchased lunch baskets at the station's market.

With their tank filled and ready for lunch, the Ripleys drove into Roswell and found the city park with playgrounds. The girls sprang from the car, screaming and skipping, followed by their excited, barking dog. Laughing, their father soon joined them, but their mother, Betty, found a shaded wooden green bench where she could watch her happy family. The date was March of 1947, and she was pregnant.

A soft breeze and the sound of distant laughter helped her relax. She placed her hands on her stomach and smiled at the thought of her unborn son, James. Finally, she leaned back, closed her eyes, and slowly fell into a trance-like sleep while the aliens watched her.

The extraterrestrials kept records of planets with life forms of interest. They had various ways of observing the activities of those life forms and occasionally sent observers. As Betty slept, the advanced beings merged her unborn son's life with one of their own.

Betty opened her eyes, wondering how long she had been sleeping. She felt good and rested and something else—something she had never felt before. Her son, the unsuspecting gifted hybrid, would grow to become an observer on Betty's doomed planet.

Chapter 1

Year 1947

James Ripley, born on Earth in the eleventh month of 1947, was a child of two worlds: a genesis hybrid of the doomed planet Earth and a distant, mature planetary civilization so advanced that it harnessed the total energy of its star and traveled throughout the Milky Way Galaxy at will.

Growing up in Utah at the base of the majestic Rocky Mountains, James had two mischievous sisters and loving parents. A carefree, happy boy, he entered East Millcreek elementary school one year early because both of his parents worked. His father built homes, and his mother was a nurse and a poet.

James felt loved, and that gave him confidence, security, and the foundation of his fondness for the Earth. His mother wrote a poem about him that hung in his room.

How big is James
Two Teddy Bears tall;
One medium bounce
Of a red rubber ball;

The length of a riddle
Plus one long laugh;
The height of two roses
(NO, two and a half)

One pussy willow
(A full-grown sprig);
Or fourteen lollipops—
That's how big—

. . .

Think of the wonders

On looking around

Twenty-nine kisses

Away from the ground!

James enjoyed grade school a little too much. He talked incessantly, so his second-grade teacher devised an evil plan and taped his mouth shut. That strategy soon ended when a large, muscular man with a loud voice visited the principal. James watched his father and hero with pure admiration. He had once told a stranger on a bus, "My dad can beat up any little kid in the neighborhood." James quickly covered his face when the man and his mother began laughing.

While the other boys played soccer and baseball and engaged in war-like snowball fights, James preferred chasing girls around the school's perimeter. The girls loved being chased and giggled with delight as they bolted outside when the recess bell rang.

One day, his favorite girl stopped abruptly and turned with her hands on her hips. "Okay, James, you caught me. What are you going to do with me?"

"What? You're supposed to be running," James said, a little frightened and confused.

"Well, I'm tired, and you're too fast. And my mom said to find out what you want. Are you going to kiss me?"

"Come on, Wendy; we're just playing tag."

"Hey, is this creep bothering you?" Sammy, a stalky third-grade bully with a round, chubby face, chest bumped James.

"Get out of here, Sammy!" Wendy yelled.

"Not until I teach this sissy girl chaser a lesson," Sammy said.

Wendy ran away and called back, "Hurry, James!"

Sammy growled, stepped forward, and threw a punch, but James stepped out of range. "Stop it, Sammy!" James yelled.

Sammy came at him again, so James ran away. Sammy chased after him, screaming with teeth showing and arms flailing. It surprised James how slow he ran. Chasing the girls was good exercise, and those girls were faster than this big bully. After three loops around the school, Sammy bent over, gasping for breath. James walked back and gave him a gentle push. Sammy fell crying, and Wendy laughed. Then she ran away, and James ran after her. *I do want to kiss her,* James thought. *I wish I knew how.*

In the sixth grade, James' parents enrolled him in Arlington Elementary, near his father's real estate office in Murray, Utah. James worked in the lunchroom for free meals, along with two other boys and a pretty girl named Darleen. After a while, Darleen became his quasi-girlfriend. They went skating together and spent time at the city library.

James found the science fiction book *Step to the Stars* by Lester del Rey. He kept the unusual book inside his desk at school. But when his teacher spotted him reading the unauthorized Sci-Fi, she took it from him. "You are not old enough to read this book! And anyway, humans will never travel to space," she scolded.

"Please, Miss Thompson, let me have my book. I'll take it home," James begged.

Miss Thompson returned the contraband to the city library the next day. Nevertheless, James found his book again and kept it in his bedroom at home until he finished the story. "Wow, Mom! They built a space station that floats around the Earth."

"You finished the entire book? I'm so proud of you," his mom said.

Now hooked on science fiction, James read more books that Miss Thompson would confiscate if she discovered them. He dared to ask if the kids could read *Miss Pickerell Goes to Mars* in class. With that, a yardstick slammed onto his desk. "Enough, James!"

A tough boy in his class named Jay fell in love with Darleen and became jealous of James. One day at recess and in front of the entire student body, Jay pushed James down a hill. James responded by saying, "Eww, jeepers, Jay. Gull."

Jay pounced. "*Eww, gee, gull,*" he mocked.

The kids laughed hysterically, and James became famous. Even his teacher laughed when she heard the kids teasing him, but she eventually told them to stop bullying. Of course, they continued with the dastardly *Eww, gee, gull.*

Jay bullied James daily, pushing and trying to goad him into fights. It became obvious to the kids that James feared Jay, which naturally encouraged more teasing. Darleen began spending time with Jay, so James lost his friend—no more skating or library adventures.

Sad and walking down State Street after school, James discovered the city gym. He wandered in, and a friendly old gentleman helped him signup for free and gave him the grand tour. The club included a boxing ring positioned directly in the center for spectator convenience. James loved the gym, but Jay and his friends eventually found his getaway and began following him. Three older black boys at the gym noticed the torture. Their favorite sports included boxing, but they were limited to sparring with each other because the other kids were afraid of them. Fed up with the cruelty, one of the boxers approached James.

"Hi, I'm Marv," the boy said.

"Oh, hi, I'm James."

"Hey, would you like to learn how to box?" Marv asked.

"Uh, well, you are too good for me."

"No, I mean, can we teach you how to box?" Marv explained.

"Yeah, sure! Would you do that?"

In two months, James could punch the speed bag with skill. Marv said he had natural fast-twitch muscles. "Dude, you are getting good!"

That day, James sprinted to his dad's office on State Street to tell him what Marv had said. His dad laughed and gave him a couple of fake punches.

One month later, Jay tracked James to the gym and bumped him as they entered the doorway. While talking to his friends, Jay spotted James practicing on the heavy bag near the boxing ring. He ran over and grabbed it with both hands. "Hey, wanna go a couple rounds with me?" Jay taunted.

"No thanks," James said and walked away, still afraid.

Marv heard the challenge and found James by the drinking fountain. "James, my man," Marv said. "You should box him. Trust me, that dude has no chance."

"Are you sure, Marv? I know he's just a bully. I don't know what's wrong with him, but he scares me."

"Yes, I'm sure, I'm very sure," Marv replied.

And so, James found Jay and held up his gloves. "Okay, Jay, I think it would be fun to box. But take it easy on me." Then he climbed into the ring.

James' three buddies scrambled to a bench near the ring, and a small crowd formed. Marv winked at James and flashed a big smile.

Utterly surprised, Jay stood by the ring as half a dozen of his pals joined the growing crowd of spectators. "Clean the EwwGee's clock!" a freckle-faced friend of Jay's told him as he helped him with his gloves and boosted him into the ring.

James' confident friends rolled off their bench in unison, laughing and dancing. The entertainment surprised Jay and attracted more kids along with two adults. One of the adults rang a bell, and the fight began.

Jay fell to the canvas after two quick jabs and a right lead. He jumped up angry and came swinging wildly. James quickly stepped to the side and ducked under the blows. As Jay turned, he faced a looping right hand from James, and down he went again.

James' friends were celebrating now and mimicking the events in the ring. James glanced over to see their antics.

This time, getting up slowly, Jay put his fists forward in an awkward, child-like pose and approached with caution. James faked another right, then, once in range, he caught Jay with two solid jabs. This time, Jay fell from the jabs. Sitting on the canvas, he pulled off his gloves and slammed them down. James wanted to say, *Eww, Gee, Gull*, but instead, he helped Jay to his feet and patted him on the back.

"There is something about you, James. I've never seen a little kid that fast. Damn, boy, I've never seen any kid that fast. Are you even human?" Marv wrapped his arm around his younger friend, and the others helped him off with his gloves.

Once more, James sprinted to his dad's store and told him about the fight while trying to catch his breath. "Marv doesn't think I'm human!"

"That is true," his dad said as he hugged him. "I've always suspected you of being the real superboy."

Days later, James had morphed into a hero at school. Darleen tried to make up, but that young epic romance was over. James knew his time in Murray would end soon, and he would miss his boxing pals the most. Close to his home on the East Bench of Salt Lake City, a brand new junior high school neared completion. It would be the next school for Earth's last hope.

Chapter 2

Rocky Mountains

James lived on the East Bench of Salt Lake City, near the base of the Rocky Mountains. Two green steel water tanks were above his home, nestled in a carved-out mountain section. James loved climbing that mountain. He would throw rocks at the water tanks from the surrounding cliffs. The sounds echoed across the neighborhood.

James could see the entire Salt Lake valley from above the tanks. He climbed like a mountain goat and preferred to hike alone. One day, his curiosity exhorted him to climb the steel ladder to the top of his favorite forty-foot tank. He piled rocks to reach the edge of the ladder, which commenced ten feet from the ground. James guessed that the ladder's high starting edge helped discourage kids from climbing the tank.

At last, James clutched the first stepping bar. It was cold, thick, and solid and protruded about a foot from the water tank itself. Pulling himself up to where both feet were on the ladder, he looked down. *Yikes!* He squeezed the bar so hard he wondered if he might break it. Slowly he made his way to the top of the tank.

Sliding on his stomach, he moved away from the edge. The smooth, hard steel top puffed toward the center to shed rainwater. After reaching the bulging center, James stood up and threw his arms toward the sky. "I'm the king of bunker's hill!" he shouted.

With courage, he walked closer to the opposite edge to see the streets and houses far below. On the nearest road, Crestwood Drive, his friend Erik sat in front of his home in his wheelchair. Erik had contracted polio two years before the Salk vaccine. James hauled his friend around the neighborhood in a wagon and pulled him on a sleigh in the winter. They were best friends.

"Hey, Erik!" James yelled.

Erik looked around and finally spotted James on the water tank waving his arms.

"Are you crazy? How did you get up there?" Erik yelled.

"This is fun! I'll be down in a while. Don't tell my mom," James yelled back.

James glanced to the right and saw his home farther away on El Rancho Road.

"Hurry, I have to show you something!" Erik yelled.

With that, James ran back toward the ladder. But as he neared the edge, he slipped, fell to his butt, and sailed off the tank. The ground came at him like an angry monster. With a loud thud, he landed. Dust surrounded him, and he couldn't breathe. But instead of dying, James became furious at the ground for walloping him.

He got up, swearing and clenching his fist. "Damn it! Damn, that hurt! Don't do that!" James yelled and stamped the ground as if punishing it.

Wow, I must be tough. He ran down the mountain and told Erik what had happened. Erik laughed and suggested that they get even with the water tank. He pulled out a bag of cherry bombs. "Let's make a cannon and shoot the green fatso," Erik said.

"Where did you get those?" James asked.

"I stole them from my brother's friend, Stephen, the jerk."

That did not surprise James. Erik possessed extraordinary mischief. "So, how do we make a cannon?"

"We take this pipe and drill a hole in the end for the fuse to fit through it. See how the end screws off and on? We put the cherry bomb in the pipe and stuff it with a steely marble and sawdust," Erik explained.

A brilliant boy—Erik had no common sense.

They worked on their weapon for two hours and then admired the masterpiece. They tied the cannon onto a wood frame and aimed it at the poor water tank over two hundred yards away.

"There is no way in hell that thing will hit the tank." Erik's big brother, Otto, stood behind them laughing.

"Do you think the tank will explode?" Erik asked.

"That's funny. Your cannon won't make it halfway."

"Well, let's try it," James said.

Erik wheeled away behind the garage. Otto lit the fuse, then he and James ran. They reached Erik as the cannon fired. The solid steel marble whistled through the air and found its target, slamming into the water tank with outrageous violence; it sounded like a bomb. The boys hid when neighbors came out of their homes to see what had happened.

Water pressure behind the steel frame prevented the cannonball from penetrating the tank. James, Erik, and Otto made a solemn oath never to build another cherry bomb cannon.

Two weeks later, Otto drove Erik, James, and Stephen to a fishing camp above Kamas, Utah, near the Provo River. Erik made the strategic mistake of bringing his stolen cherry bombs. Stephen spotted them, snatched them away, and pushed Erik into a mud puddle.

James lifted his friend out of the water and yelled at Stephen, "Hey bitch, if I throw a stick, will you chase it?"

With that, Stephen came after James, but Otto stopped him. Stephen turned and stomped off with his cherry bombs. Otto warned the two misfits that he could not always protect them and chased after Stephen.

With a wide grin, Erik pulled out a cherry bomb he had stashed in his side pocket. "Don't light that!" James pleaded.

"I won't. Here, you keep it safe."

Hours later, James noticed Stephen enter the campground's lone outhouse. "There goes stinky," he said to Erik.

"I wish I could light the cherry by that outhouse," Erik said.

James walked toward the metal porta-potty and looked at the air vent on top. He pointed to the vent and said, "Should we scare the hell out of him?"

Erik clenched his fist, bounced in his chair, and rapidly nodded.

"The metal shaft will keep him from getting hurt. Give me a match and go hide in those trees."

James snuck up on the outhouse and heard Stephen mumbling about one of his *Playboy* magazines. James found a log and quietly placed it on the air vent side. Terrified, he stood on the unstable wood, lit the cherry bomb, and dropped it down the vent.

Expecting a loud bang, James heard a bloop and a splatter, followed by, "Eww, shit!"

James burst out laughing and ran for his life. Erik could never have reached the air vent, so he remained relatively safe. But James knew he needed another way home.

It took Stephen ten minutes to wipe the crap off his butt; by then, James was long gone. Luckily for James, his family had a log cabin about three miles away in the Soapstone area. James jogged the entire distance. Approaching, he saw his Uncle George outside chopping wood. James told his uncle what he had done and begged for a ride home.

Uncle George continued laughing until he pulled into the driveway an hour later. James' mother smiled while standing in the kitchen window. She waved at George and held up cookies on a tray. With that, George turned off his car and went inside with James. Betty's homemade oatmeal cookies were famous and irresistible.

After James graduated from high school with a D average, his general counselor ordered him to avoid college. So naturally, James signed up for night school at the University of Utah. Later, Utah accepted him into day school after he made a 4.0 in his first quarter at night school and passed his SAT.

The review board told James his SAT score rocketed off the charts. Half the applicants admitted to Carnegie Mellon University had SAT scores between 1460 and 1560. James had an unexplainable score of 1550.

James found classes at night interesting and less restrictive. For algebra, he entered a dimly lit room on the second floor of the famous old math building. "What are you doing here?" a familiar voice shouted.

"Slaughter!" James replied in surprise. "Are you teaching this night gig?"

Mr. Slaughter was a former boxer and a high school math teacher at Skyline High School in Salt Lake City, Utah. He had an unusual twitch as he worked his equations on the chalkboard. He also had a teaching technique of saying, "Now you say to yourself," as if that would help solve every math problem.

James had spent most of his time in algebra at Skyline, being sent to the hall for misbehaving. One day, Slaughter asked him to explain an equation to the class. James walked to the board with a puzzled expression and began, "Now you say to yourself...Self!"

Laughter exploded from the class, and Slaughter did his best to hide a grin as he exiled poor James once more to the hall. Mr. Slaughter liked James.

On the twenty-second day of November 1963, James stood alone in the hall listening to the loudspeaker as the death of President John F. Kennedy was announced. Filled with grief and anger, he slugged the wall. At the end of the empty hall, a teacher turned toward the echoing sounds but said nothing.

James walked down the same hall toward the teacher and out of the building. Behind him, an increasing rumble of excited students filled the air. The sounds of crying. The sounds of screaming. The sounds of commotion. The sounds of chaos faded as he ran for a nearby orchard. He inhaled the smell and bit into a hard tear-stained green apple.

"I've been working up here for a couple of years," Mr. Slaughter explained. "I thought Budge, your counselor, told you not to bother with college. So again, what are you doing here?"

"Yeah, well, Mr. Budge was never too fond of me. I told him in a packed assembly that his zipper was down. The man had no gratitude."

"Oh, I heard about that. But I still have a problem. You managed to flunk my algebra class twice. So, what makes you think you can pass this advanced college class?" Mr. Slaughter walked closer as other students filled the room with typical chatter. He grabbed James' arm and took him aside for a private conversation.

"Well, I'm hoping I can stay in the classroom long enough to enjoy the benefits of your famous teaching skills," James said with a stupid-ass grin.

"You behave, and we will get along just fine, son. I'm on your side. Honestly, I'm pleased to see you here."

At the end of the quarter, Mr. Slaughter cornered his worst-ever high school student and gave him a big bear hug. "James, when you become curious, you light up. I've never seen anything like it. Stay curious."

"Awkward!" James declared as he hugged back. He never saw Mr. Slaughter again, but he often thought of him.

James spent the next few years working summer jobs and attending class. He owned a crenulated 1963 Mercury, Comet that his dad had bought him. His car had a broken window on the back driver's side door that he patched with clear plastic and duct tape.

His two favorite subjects were philosophy and physics. The questions he had for those poor teachers were never-ending.

Wanting to visit the islands, he landed a summer gig as a surf instructor in Honolulu, Hawaii, by faking his resume. He arrived early, with no experience, but learned how to surf in two weeks, thanks to a friend named Anuhea. Surf teaching became tedious but bearably amusing. It required standing waist-high in ocean water, attempting to launch out-of-shape tourists onto a two-foot wave. But at least he had the benefit of surfing after work.

One afternoon, he found himself gunning a heavy wave on the North Shore Banzai Pipeline. James enjoyed the ride until he made the mistake of looking up. His right hand touched the force of the green room in a forty-foot barrel. Becoming disoriented, he wiped out.

The wave took him down a long distance from shore. James struggled against the pressure, and he thought he would never surface. Finally, his face hit soft sand near the beach, and he pushed up, gasping for air. After crawling to shore, he wandered up the coast toward a crowd of people huddled with his friend, Anuhea. She appeared to be crying, and strangers were comforting her.

"What's up?" James interrupted.

Anuhea jumped up and ran into his arms. "Are you all right?" she screamed.

"Oh, I wiped out on that monster. Why are you crying?"

"I thought you were gone. You've been under for thirty minutes!" Anuhea exclaimed.

"No, I was under a long time, but not that long. That's impossible. I have gritty sand in my mouth and nose from hitting the beach with my eyes shut."

"You're worried about the sand in your mouth?" Anuhea laughed. "Dude, you drowned!"

Soon the lifeguards had him down. They explained that news reports classified the wave as the biggest of the year. Eventually, James struggled free, and the crowd of worried onlookers gradually dispersed.

"I'm starving. Come on, Anuhea, let's get some food."

"Did you see where my surfboard landed?" James asked.

Walking, they spotted his board onshore near the peer, broken in half. "Wow, that wave was harsh!" Anuhea said.

They picked up the pieces and went back to the parking lot.

Was I truly under for thirty minutes? James wondered.

Before they left, James turned back to look again at the massive waves. A girl stood staring at James from beyond the parking lot on a wet rock cliff. Her face seemed familiar, as if he knew her from some distant memory or a dream. He glanced at Anuhea and then back at the mysterious girl, but she was gone.

Chapter 3

Mercury

In 1969, James accepted a summer job as a student electrical engineer for the Reynolds Engineering company in Mercury, Nevada. Mercury served as civilian headquarters for the Nevada Atomic Test Site.

The student engineers were assigned trailers with residents already working at Mercury, but James' roommate never appeared. The name of his trailer mate, as listed on the cork board in the main office, read: *Edwin Eugene Aldrin Jr*.

It so happened that Apollo astronauts spent time training at the Atomic Test Site because the craters were surprisingly similar to those on the Moon. When NASA made several announcements about

Apollo 11, James finally realized that his missing roommate was the astronaut Buzz Aldrin.

After work, James spent time in a full-sized hangar converted into a basketball court. The other players were also college students, and most were good athletes. James and another student engineer from the University of Utah, Tabor Austen, picked up a game with two football players, Whittingham and Bowden. They were all friends, but James only knew the football players by their last names. James and Tabor were famously undefeated as a team. After winning again, James walked over, picked up the ball, and turned to leave. As he turned, a frustrated Whittingham slugged him in the mouth.

Tabor jumped between James and the two football players and yelled at them loudly enough to attract the attention of a base military guard. Then he turned and pointed. "James! Your teeth!"

James felt his mouth; his two front teeth were bent back. He and Tabor ran for the locker room. James turned back to Whittingham and yelled, "Thafns!"

Staring at James's teeth, Tabor said, "You have double front teeth! You're like a shark or something."

"Holf on," James slurred.

He slowly pushed his four front teeth back into position as Tabor cringed.

"I read somewhere that you should straighten bent teeth right away, or they will die," James said, now able to pronounce "th" again.

"Wow. Well, you look pretty good except for the blood, and you sound fine. Let's go find some mouthwash."

Whittingham never apologized, and James quit playing basketball with the jocks. He spent more time in the desert by himself. He volunteered to measure the resistance of the ground wires attached to the power line poles spread out on the base.

The Mercury test site had almost a thousand atomic bomb circles splattered across the desert. The last open-air blast exploded in 1962, with the radiation declared safe by 1969. They called that last bomb *Little Feller*.

Curious and meddlesome, James began researching the history of the atomic test site. He had access to an assortment of non-public documents. He learned about Project Sedan, a shallow underground nuclear test conducted in Area 10 of the Yucca Flats on Jul 6, 1962. The blast was part of Operation Plowshare, a program to investigate the use of nuclear weapons for mining, cratering, and other civilian purposes

They planned to see how big of a hole they could blow into the Earth. It worked, but Sedan resulted in a radioactive cloud that separated into two plumes rising 10,000 ft and 16,000 ft. The two dust clouds headed northeast, then turned east in roughly parallel paths towards the Atlantic Ocean. Releasing 880,000 curies of radioactive iodine-131, an evil agent that causes thyroid disease and cancer, Sedan killed over 30,000 Americans, but it would take years before the government revealed the truth.

On Jul 20, 1969, the alien hybrid found the site of Sedan. As he dangled his feet over the massive crater, the Apollo 11 landing module descended toward the Moon. He heard an excited Walter Cronkite describing the landing from the full-volume truck radio below. The eagle had landed!

I'm witnessing the best and the worst of humanity today, he thought. James took a deep breath and leaned back on his elbows. The massive crater appeared surreal. It looked like a giant insect had flown down from space and dug a vast, perfect cone into the surface of the Earth. He laughed at the absurdity of why anyone would want to do this. "What good is it?" he asked out loud.

"No good. So why are you admiring this worthless hole?" The voice from behind sounded like a young woman.

James scrambled to his feet and spun around, almost stumbling backward into the giant crater. A partially transparent hologram of a young, trim woman floated near the ground before him. She had long, straight, light brown hair and wore a blue and white checkered button-up blouse with dark, tight-fitting shorts. She appeared dressed for hiking, and her left wrist held a thick unusual bracelet.

"What? I mean, what is this? Who are you?" James asked.

The woman glanced at her bracelet, then replied, "I am sorry for surprising you. Call me Juni. We came here to observe your adventure. Traveling to another world for the first time is an achievement worth documenting." "Well, I mean, what are you? Where did you come from?" James asked again as he moved away from the crater's edge with a glance backward.

"From these bomb craters, it is apparent that you are a violent species. Do you enjoy blowing holes in this planet?" the lady asked in a disarmingly calm and pleasant voice.

"Uh, no. I was just sitting here listening to the Moon landing. I don't understand the purpose of this dumb, worthless hole either," James replied.

"Then why are you here instead of on your Moon?"

"Well, I would love to be on the Moon right now, but I'm just a kid. I mean, I'm a student engineer. I kinda got stuck with this gig. But I don't understand what's happening. How did you get here? Are you a projection from Area 51?"

"I have one question, James Ripley. Would you prefer exploring the Moon and beyond, or would you prefer making these dangerous weapons?" the attractive hologram lady still had a pleasant way about her.

"I would prefer exploring space! I love the space program," James said as he approached the lady's image. "But how do you know my name?"

"We met once before, in San Francisco. Until later, James. We will have more questions for you in the future." Instantly, the hologram disappeared.

"Wait! Come back!" James yelled.

To his utter astonishment, the young lady reappeared. "I'm sorry. Did you have something important to tell me?"

For the first time in his life, James Ripley was speechless.

"It's all right, James. We will meet again, I promise." Goodbye for now." Juni disappeared once again.

James gathered his gear and stumbled down the crater's rim to his truck. It seemed odd now that he had no walkie-talkie. *If the people running this base can transmit talking holograms, why no simple com-device for the engineers out here in the desert?*

By the time James returned that Sunday night, the Mercury base seemed abandoned. He made his way to the lone cafeteria, shining like a beacon in the dark. The inexperienced electrical engineer designing the new café lighting system had made a minor two-fold error in his foot-candle calculations. But James' mistake could only be seen at night, and his boss was never there after 5 P.M.

A television hung outside the café, about twenty feet up. Two remaining spectators watched the Moon Landing as Armstrong prepared to exit the capsule. He thought about telling them of his strange encounter, but they were too absorbed in the extraordinary events playing out on the dangling monitor. The entire planet stood still, thrilled with the adventure, yet the utter unknown was frightening—the Earth held its breath.

James thought about the girl and the hologram and wondered if someone else, not from Earth, might be on the Moon observing. "That would be more than weird," James blurted, but no one noticed.

He watched Neil Armstrong climbing down the ladder and onto the surface of the Moon.

"That's one small step for **a** man, one giant leap for mankind." NASA later changed what Armstrong said to "That's one small step for man, one giant leap for mankind."

With amazement, he experienced the entire Moon-walk with Armstrong and Aldrin. As he wandered back to his trailer alone in the warm desert air, he had a dangerous tempting idea.

Rising early, James headed to the vast parking lot of new pickup trucks. *Why are hundreds of new, unused vehicles parked and gleaming in the desert? What is their purpose?* James found his favorite truck, having tried a dozen already. Then he drove north up Mercury highway through the Atomic Test Site. James, the spy, would turn onto Groom Lake Road and then find the back entrance to Area

51 at gate 700. With his handy detailed map, he knew the journey would be about 50 miles each way from Mercury.

This route remained unavailable to the public, but James had seen workers at Area 51 make the same trek to and from Las Vegas. They often waved at him. James approached Station 700, the third primary gate into Area 51. He glanced at the small, rusty OFF LIMITS sign as he passed through. Next, he drove beyond his familiar Sedan Crater and found Groom Lake Road. Finally, he headed toward a group of buildings. His Ford pickup looked precisely like the hundreds of others on the base.

He had his badge on the left side of his shirt for easy visibility. He could see a wide gate crossing the dirt road as he approached. One rather permanent and dilapidated building sat close to the entrance. Several guards were next to a pair of smaller buildings.

The guards seemed almost disinterested as he approached. James raised his left hand out the window and waved. One of the guards walked forward as the gate swung open. Then he waved back and retreated. James drove through the gate past a large sign that read:

WARNING – MILITARY INSTALLATION – OFF LIMITS TO UNAUTHORIZED PERSONNEL

James smiled at the station guards and proceeded up the dusty road toward a mountainous area. After crossing the mountain range, he spotted a dry lake on the other side. Groom Lake is nestled next to the Area 51 Air Force base. Entering the station, he found a large parking lot on the left side and pulled in.

Chapter 4

Area 51

The air scorched on that day in 1969 when James Ripley entered Area 51. Leaving his air-conditioned truck, James hiked in the dry desert heat toward a cluster of airplane hangars.

When he entered the first one, a cool gust of air gave him sweet relief. The large building looked almost empty, but a half-dozen men surrounded two small aircraft. The planes were unusual and futuristic, with wings tilted back and designed for speed.

James left the first hangar and wandered past two others. Inside the fourth stood a mysterious round-bellied plane with the markings A-12. He wanted to spend more time with the A-12 but instead moved on, hoping to find the hologram girl.

Then he came to the largest hangar with a sign that read "Advanced Digital Systems." Spotting a small opening, he slid in. A torn banner hung crooked on a ceiling beam, showing the tattered words "Welcome to Dreamland."

In the far-left corner, a large screen appeared to show a video taken from an aircraft. Several men and two women were at consoles that reminded him of the DEC computer monitors in the University of Utah Computer Science department. A large man with a security badge approached and asked James if he worked for Evans & Sutherland.

Before James could answer, another man with an elongated head popped out from behind the big screen like a jack in the box. The sudden appearance caused James to jump back.

Then the peculiar man spoke, "According to his badge, he is from the University of Utah."

"Hello, James," he said as he shuffled closer.

"Everyone around here seems to know my name," James responded.

"Your badge has an ID number, son. You work for Reynolds."

"Oh, so that's how she knew me, the hologram girl."

Suddenly the man moved even closer, examining James like a curious monkey. "How long have you been here?"

"Oh, I just got here half an hour ago. What is that machine? Is this where they send the hologram images from?"

"They call me J-Rod. I am excited to meet you, James Ripley."

"Oh, well, um, I'm pleased to meet you, also. Have you seen the pretty girl from the hologram department?"

A noise emanated from the man that sounded almost like laughter. "No, she is not here. This device is a flight simulator, not a hologram projection system. But feel free to look around."

"Do you know where I might find her?" James asked.

"Where did you meet this girl?"

"In the desert at the Sedan Crater. She was a projection, a transparent hologram."

"You have no idea who you are, do you?" asked J-Rod.

"Sure, I do. It's not that hot outside," James said, with strain in his voice. "I'm a student engineer from The U working a summer gig!" After a short pause, James continued, "Sorry, dude, that was abrupt."

"James, feel free to explore the Groom Lake. If you encounter any problems here, say you are with J-Rod."

James spent the rest of the day hiking around the base. He found an underground train that he rode to a large cafeteria with free food. He met pilots and even an Air Force four-star general. Scientists and tech workers seemed eager to meet him. It made no sense. *I guess knowing J-Rod is a big deal* here, James thought.

As he prepared to leave, a young man with thick glasses ran up to him, gasping for breath. "Hey, do you want to see something?"

"What?" James asked.

"The Roswell Saucer," the man replied. "The one from 1947."

Stunned, James had believed the alien crash was a publicity stunt. No one had ever seen a real UFO.

"They have an actual alien spacecraft here?" James asked.

The young man seemed surprised. "Follow me," he shouted and dashed toward a round tunnel entrance.

James caught up as the man dropped his nerd glasses. James snatched them up and handed them back to the excited boy. They entered the tunnel and walked along a dimly lit hall at a slight downward slope. The journey lasted about ten minutes before they entered a room that looked more like a museum than an air-force base.

James kept pace with the eager young man as they passed several large glass enclosures containing objects that James could not identify. They turned and entered another room. There, in the middle, floated a large round craft about fifty yards in diameter. Both men and women were examining the object with various equipment. One brave man balanced on top, looking around. James had a rare feeling of déjà vu.

"We still can't get inside. All the stories about dead aliens are false. We don't know what is inside. Even J-Rod can't break the security." A tall, slender woman leaned next to James, explaining. The young nerd character had left.

"It's extremely light. We had no problem bringing it here. But the material is impervious. We can't even see inside with X-rays."

James walked to the craft and could not resist touching it. The surface felt like glass and cool to the touch.

"Can you help us get inside?" the woman asked.

"Me? No, I'm just visiting. I'm a student engineer working out of Mercury. It's way beyond anything I could help with," James replied. "This thing is incredible."

"I just thought that because J-Rod, the alien, told everyone to give you the grand tour, you might be able to help," the lady explained.

"J-Rod is an alien? Oh boy, this day just keeps getting weirder. No, sorry, I'm just a student from Utah. I have no idea why he likes me."

"Well, he won't admit he's an alien, but he sure knows a lot." The woman seemed disappointed. "Would you mind following me to the saucer entrance? I think you might find this intriguing."

James followed her to a location on the craft where a hand indent flashed visible on the surface. "It looks like whoever built this was human, not alien," James said.

"Please put your hand in the door lock. Don't be afraid; it's never harmed, anyone."

"Okay, sure." James reached over and placed his hand into the imprint. He felt a surge run through his body, but nothing happened to the craft. The frustrated woman frowned and strutted away with not even a goodbye.

As evening approached, a friendly pilot asked James if he wanted a ride back to Mercury. James explained that he had driven there in a company truck. A woman with the pilot took notes on a curious handheld device. She assured James that the vehicle would not be a problem. James knew plenty of other trucks identical to his were at Mercury, so he accepted a helicopter ride.

Upon arrival, he thanked the pilot, sprinted from the landing pad to his friend Tabor's trailer, and pounded on the door, but no one answered. Too tired to wait, he headed back. Walking, he sensed someone following him. With goosebumps on his neck, James quickly stepped out of the street lights near the side of a building. Then he waited in the dark for his stalker.

The man who walked past carried a gun. Guns were not legal in Mercury. Once the stranger walked out of sight, James ran to the security station and told them about the stalker. An officer took him to an interrogation room. An older officer entered and identified himself as a captain. He explained to James that the man following him was a government agent. Then he asked James why he returned on a helicopter.

Before James could answer, another soldier entered the room and whispered something to the captain. The captain turned and said, "Sorry to hear about your truck. You were lucky the pilot spotted you."

All the soldiers left, so James found his way outside. When he finally returned to his trailer, he saw Tabor waiting for him on the metal steps. "Where have you been, dude?" Tabor shouted.

Tabor remained silent as James told him all about his Area 51 adventure. The two friends entered the trailer, and James collapsed into a chair as Tabor raided the small fridge. "We need to get out of here, James. That agent you saw came to my trailer and gave me the once over."

"What? What did he want?" James asked.

"Oh, just about everything. I mean, it was spooky. You stirred something up. These guys know you were out there."

"Yeah, I think you're right. And I've been getting flak for my research into that Sudan project. Hey, a friend of mine said there is a big music concert with a war protest planned, and he's in one of the bands. Should we go?"

"Sure. That sounds fun. Where is it at?" Tabor asked with his head still in the fridge.

"Well, it's in the southern part of New York near a place called Woodstock," James replied.

"That's a long way. When is this concert?"

"We need to be there by the 15th of next month. So, we could give our two-week notice and see if my 63 Mercury Comet can get us there."

"If they have girls, count me in. This place is bad for my love life," Tabor said as he handed James an apple.

"There's probably no girls, but my friend, Bruce, was psyched."

"A music festival with no girls. That's funny, dude. Let's go!"

James and Tabor planned their trip to Woodstock with no idea what they would find. Back at Area 51, the entrance to the alien spacecraft opened for the first time since 1947. Then it closed again with five people still inside, including J-Rod.

Chapter 5

Woodstock

James and Tabor arrived in New York on Friday morning, August 15, 1969. Scattered cars filled the streets like dominos. Instead of fighting the traffic, the adventurous duo parked their Comet near the corner of 17B in Monticello, grabbed their backpacks and tent, and embarked on their hike to the dairy farm in Bethel. They needed exercise after the long drive, so the trek felt good. James' friend, Bruce, told them to bring a tent. It turned out to be good advice.

After almost eleven miles, they spotted the gathering. By noon there were thousands of kids. There were no restroom facilities, and the grounds on the 600-acre farm splashed wet from the rain. Over 50,000 early arrivals had already purchased the food at the concession stands. While standing alone, some friendly kids approached and claimed to feel good vibes from the rain-soaked travelers. Their circle of hippies offered to share their food and drinks.

A posted concert billing nearby said, "Aquarian Exposition: 3 Days of Peace & Music." The smells and sounds of so many people were overwhelming at first. Later, the boys found a spot on the outer edge of the crowd and pitched their tent.

In less than thirty minutes, two college girls found them. They were standing in the rain with pouty faces; heads hung low and cute as could be, so naturally, Tabor invited them into the small tent.

The girls were from nearby SUNY Sullivan, a public community college in Loch Sheldrake, New York. After the rain stopped, the four walked past the concert stands to a farm pond occupied by laughing kids. The girls took off all their clothes and jumped into the small lake screaming as they hit the water.

"You have to come in," Katy yelled. The other girl's name was Melanie.

"Why not?" Tabor yelled back, and the boys stripped down to their underwear. There were children in the area, or they would have gone naked.

After bathing and giving each other tight hugs, the four dressed and returned to the concert. Tabor strolled through heaven, Woodstock heaven.

Richie Havens appeared on stage as the massive crowd settled onto the damp ground. Melanie snuggled up to James, and Katy found Tabor's warm arms. A humble guru from India gave the opening speech. Hindu Swami Satchidananda told the young crowd that the world's future belonged to them.

Governor Rockefeller had gathered 10,000 troops to disburse the visitors but changed his mind as the crowd grew to hundreds of thousands.

The swami explained to the crowd of future yoga hippies, the flower children, that music is the celestial sound that controls the entire universe. The government began spreading rumors about the damn stupid hippies, calling them draft dodgers and troublemakers high on drugs. But the swami offered his teachings as a way to escape drugs. In truth, the crowd of 500,000 consisted mainly of intelligent college students.

In the afternoon, the four friends joined the large crowd for a better view of Joan Baez as she sang, "Oh, Happy Day."

This is fun, James thought. He believed everything happening might possibly be historic.

Then he saw her! Juni moved fifteen feet in front of him, dressed as a hippie.

James wormed his way through the horde until he found her. "So, you are real," James said.

Tabor managed to follow his friend. As Juni turned toward him, James reached close to her arm and said, "I'd like you to meet my friend, Tabor."

"Who is this goddess? Is she human?" Tabor asked.

"What? What do you mean?" James turned, surprised by Tabor's reaction.

"Meet me by the pond," Juni yelled and fled through the crowd.

"I have to follow her, Tabor. That's the girl, the hologram girl. Tell the girls I ran into an old friend." James left and struggled to follow Juni. When he reached the pond, he saw her knee-deep in water.

"We meet again, James Ripley."

"How did you know I was here? How did you get here from Area 51?" James asked.

"I was never at Area 51, James. I was never physically at that atomic crater either," Juni responded with her charming smile.

"Well, where did you project your holographic image from, then?"

"Our space vessel. We were orbiting the Moon to watch the first human land there," Juni replied.

"Holy Moses! So, are you an alien?" James asked, realizing his dumb question.

"You catch on fast, James," Juni said sarcastically.

"How did you know I was here?"

"I didn't know you were here. When we saw the large gathering for peace, I felt compelled. I had to see this in person because humans are so combative."

"Well, it's some coincidence that we should meet again, don't you think?"

"Yes, that is some coincidence. Do you have a question for me?" Juni asked.

"Oh, I have a million questions for you. I don't know where to begin."

"Well, when you think of one, let's meet again," Juni responded.

"Quit teasing me," James said. "Do all aliens look like humans?"

"Do you think this is what I look like?" Juni asked.

"I do. I saw the hand imprint on the 1947 spacecraft at Area 51. It's a human imprint." James said, proud of his quick thinking.

"You have been busy, James Ripley. I think you might be the curious type after all."

"In truth, we built that spacecraft for you, for humans. It would not be my first choice for interstellar space travel."

"Okay, if you are not human, can I see what you look like?" James asked.

"You don't like the way I look? Your friend Tabor seemed to enjoy my appearance," Juni said with a smile.

"Well, yeah, I think you're cute, but I'm wondering what I'm dealing with here. Are you a lizard?"

Juni smiled with a twinkle in her eyes. "No, I'm not a lizard, James. Now, do you have a real question for me?"

"Why are you here? Why did you build that spacecraft for us? Nobody can get inside, and it's been here for years."

"James, I have to leave again. But perhaps you should be asking—why are we here talking to you?" Juni's voice faded solemn.

"What? Wait! Don't go. Can I ask just one more question?"

"Of course, James Ripley. Ask one more question."

"Is the Earth in danger?"

"Not from us, James. We will meet again."

At that moment, Tabor and the girls came running. "Where's the girl?" Tabor shouted.

"Oh, she had to leave. She does that a lot," James said.

James and Tabor remained for all three days of the festival. Finally, James relaxed and enjoyed the moment. In the end, they said goodbye to the girls and headed back to the car.

On the way home, James told Tabor about his talk with Juni. Tabor advised him not to mention the story to anyone else, or they might lock him up in the Provo Loony Bin. James dropped Tabor off at his home in Holliday and drove to his parent's house above Wasatch Boulevard and 33rd South. He parked his car, and his old black Labrador tackled him to the grass in the front yard. His dog, Zed, squirmed, overcome with excitement.

While lying on the grass, his mom came outside to see him. "Did you do anything fun this summer?" she asked.

James laughed, and Zed attacked him again. He stood and wrapped his arms around his mom and gave her a long hug.

I need to find out why Earth is in danger, James thought as he hugged his mom and petted jealous Zed.

Chapter 6

Computer Science

While walking the halls of the Merrill Engineering Building, James noticed a busy seminar starting. The makeshift sign said, "*Computer Science Will Change the World.*" As an electrical engineering student, he shared the same building with the CS students, but James had wondered about this new science.

Curious, he entered the room and found a seat. The Professor, Evans, approached the center stage and tapped the microphone. James stood to escape the room filled with nerds when something caught his attention. On a screen behind the professor rotated a spacecraft. The ship floated on the screen, but not exactly like a video.

"Many of you in this room will live to see the Earth connected by computers. There will be instant communication from anywhere in the world. Your computers will become much smaller, and they will talk to other computers. You will become the builders of a new global network."

James sat back down. The professor nodded at him. Professor Evans spoke clear English, but James understood little of what the professor lectured. Even the terminology eluded him. Still, James became convinced that this was indeed important. The next day James changed his major from Electrical Engineering to Computer Science.

James developed a fascination with his computer classes. He seemed to have a knack for programming. A course by Professor Sutherland used a book entitled *Electronic Digital Systems*, written by R.K. Richards. Far into the future, software developers would continue to reference this book. The original computer scientists, like Richards, must have found mystical inspiration from somewhere, as if they were serving a muse that knew the future.

James consumed dozens of books on computer technology, but he knew he had something special when he got hold of *Electronic Digital Systems*. The other books were limited to studies of specific computers or one-chapter presentations on various topics like circuits and applications. But pedagogically, this book illustrated more clarity than case studies. It covered computing history, stored programs, automatic programming, digital data transmission (internet), and telephone messages (mobile devices). It even covered computers that think (AI).

"Why did you give my program an F?" James asked Professor Davidson, who taught the programming class on 3D models.

"Because it won't work. It makes no sense," the professor replied.

"Why don't we give it a try?" James asked.

"No, that would be a waste of computer resources. I can't do that."

At that moment, James understood a fundamental truth about computer programming. If it works, it works!

The professor had no idea that his student had come in late to work on his project. James bribed the operators for time on the DEC-10 with irresistible junk food.

The simple computer graphics assignment needed to display a rotating cube. James did not like the technique taught by Professor Davidson, so he wrote a new algorithm that used a quarter of the code and executed much faster.

Two days later, on a Friday night, James left his application running on a computer and found a couch outside the computer room. He knew Davidson worked weekends on a project. Up all night, James waited for Davidson. When he entered the computer room, James quietly followed him. By luck, Davidson sat at the same computer running James' code.

The professor reached up to abort the program when James spoke up from behind. "It works, Professor."

Davidson spun around to see James standing there with a big grin.

"What works? What are you doing here, James?"

"Just testing my program. If you look, that's the same code you said couldn't work."

The Professor turned around and tapped on the keyboard. The programming code flashed up on the CRT. He scrolled through and finally relaunched the application. "This is impossible! It's only three pages. This code makes no sense."

"I've made an amazing discovery," James said. "If it works, it works. Ain't that great about computers!"

James explained his code to the mesmerized professor for the next half hour. On Monday, a printout of the application sat on James' desk with a big A written on it.

Over time, James gained the attention of Evans & Sutherland. Together, they launched a startup in 1968 by the same name. A weathered shack housed their headquarters, and now they wanted to hire James. But James had received a different job offer and declined the Evans & Sutherland proposal for being too risky. James was great at science and not too clever at business. Evans & Sutherland eventually became an enormous success in the early field of *Computer Graphics*.

While studying physics, a Computer Science prerequisite, James discovered the lectures and writings by Caltech professor Richard Feynman. Feynman received the Nobel Prize in Physics in 1966 for his fundamental work in quantum electrodynamics. Called "The Great Explainer," Feynman could teach physics to his undergraduate students in a way that both captured their attention and made complex subjects understandable. His book, *The Feynman Lectures on Physics*, published in 1963, had simplicity, beauty, and unity. It became the most popular book on physics ever written.

The third volume in the book covered quantum mechanics and made famous the double-slit experiment. A feeling of déjà vu enveloped James while studying the double-slit experiment. *Why did he care so much about quantum mechanics?*

Quantum mechanics is the study of infinitesimal things. It explains the behavior of matter's interactions with energy on atomic and subatomic particles. By contrast, standard physics and the theory of relativity explain matter and energy on a scale familiar to humans, including the behavior of astronomical bodies such as planets.

James found quantum entanglement most interesting because particles separated by any distance exhibit the same properties; if one property changes, so do the properties in the other entangled particle. Entanglement flew in the face of Einstein's theory that nothing could exceed the speed of light. If entanglement exists, perhaps faster-than-light speed travel is possible. And that would explain how Juni, an alien from another star system, could visit the Earth. James would be ready for her the next time they met. *Was quantum entanglement the way she traveled between the stars?*

Einstein considered entanglement impossible because it violated his local realism. He called the theory "spooky." But still, Juni traveled to Earth. *How did she get here?*

James had another question. *Could a quantum computer be built?* The potential for that kind of computer would be almost unlimited.

On a clear night, the full Moon lit the Wasatch mountains. The sprinklers came on as James walked back from the Physics building to his car in the northeast student parking lot. He sprinted to escape a soaking, then continued his walk across the large open lawn next to the Einar Nielsen Fieldhouse.

Suddenly, Juni appeared again. The holographic image looked so clear and colorful this time that James thought for a moment that it was Juni in person—the same Juni he had met at Woodstock.

"Juni!" James yelled as he approached. He glanced around to make sure they were alone.

"Hello, James. Have you been thinking about me?"

"I have indeed. I have important questions for you."

"As always, I am here for you, James."

"Juni, are you using quantum entanglement to achieve space travel?"

"Well, that is an interesting question, James. Why do you ask?"

"I've been studying quantum physics and thought it might be a possibility."

"Let me check," Juni replied. Five seconds later, she answered. "We use what you might call quantum tunneling."

"Wow! That is incredible," James said. "Could quantum physics be used to build more advanced computers?"

"You are curious tonight, James. The answer, of course, is yes. But you must understand and accept the fundamental truth that Earth will not survive long enough to reach that level of advancement," Juni said in a quiet, almost sad voice.

"Then why are you here?" James asked.

"Only to observe. We will not interfere in the natural progress of this planet."

"But you already have," James said as he thought to himself, *checkmate.*

"No, James, we cannot interfere. We cannot change Earth's destiny."

"But I can," James responded.

"James, you are here as an observer and nothing more. You must provide an accurate record of the history of Earth. I can assure you that you cannot change the destiny of Earth's destruction."

"Then help me, Juni. Tell me what will happen to Earth. Together we might be able to save her."

"James, keep studying, keep learning as much as you can. You are helping us produce a complete record of this planet. We must record the lessons learned from her history. We must record the hopes and failures and the progress of humanity. All history is valuable. We will meet again, James Ripley." In a flash, Juni disappeared.

Well, that sucks, James thought. *I need to find out what the hell is going on.*

Chapter 7

Lost Love

"You look like a smart guy. Why are you reading that crap?"

James spun around aggressively, ready for a confrontation. But instead, he found himself facing a stunning young girl dressed in hippie clothes.

A girl from Woodstock? She had long, dark hair, sparkling eyes, and a sexy figure sculptured by yoga exercises. She had a sunflower in her hair and held a yoga mat on her hip. *That smile,* James thought. *That smile could launch a thousand wars.*

"What's wrong, flyboy? Cat got your tongue?" the girl asked.

After staring too long, James recovered, "Why do you call me 'flyboy'?"

"Naval Academy lit?"

James glanced down at his article on becoming a navy pilot. "Busted. It seems to be the only way to space, and I have to get there," James said, still mesmerized.

"Okay, so you want to go bomb rice farmers, got it." The girl turned to leave.

"Wait, what's your name?" James called out.

"Alice, like Alice in Wonderland. Why do you want to know?"

"I'd like to talk about it. Which part is crap?" James asked.

"The Vietnam war statistics. It's all crap," said Alice.

James picked up the newspaper sitting open on a war news page. "They need good pilots to stop the communist expansion," James explained.

"As I said, you look like a smart guy. If you believe the enemy kill claims, the US military has already wiped out the entire North Vietnam army three times. It's all lies."

"Okay, I can see you need some friendly education. This war is needed to free the people of Vietnam. And by the way, I was at Woodstock, so I understand all the hippie opposition."

"You were at Woodstock? Alice asked, moving closer.

"Yep, good music and bad girls dressed like you." James regretted that statement. "I'm sorry, that was rude. I'm an idiot."

"Tell me about Woodstock. I so wanted to be there," Alice pleaded, ignoring the apology.

"It was fun. It was crazy. To be honest, I loved it," James said.

"But nothing sunk in? You are still a war hawk?"

"I need to become an astronaut. I can't explain why," James said with conviction.

"So, you are willing to kill innocent people to become an astronaut?" Alice looked dead serious now.

"I'll be honest, the kids at Woodstock were anything but stupid," James said. "But would you be willing to let me convince you of the truth? I think the war is necessary."

"Sure, let's meet here again tomorrow, same time. I have a class, or I'd shake some sense into you right now."

For the next two weeks, James studied everything he could find on the war, and an epic internal struggle ensued. His boyhood self had believed the cowboys were the good guys, not the Indians, and now he thought the US military would save the planet. But his research and his arguments with Alice were not working. Alice was brilliant and convincing, and James felt the pain of losing his convictions. "You are a curious one," Alice said one day. "Stay curious, James."

James felt his cognitive dissonance dissolving.

Devastated, he called and asked Alice to meet him by the old Physics building. The sun began setting when he saw her. She approached with her usual beautiful smile and a few skips and twirls. James had tears in his eyes. What's wrong, James?" Alice asked

"You are right. I can't do this. I'm withdrawing my application to the Naval Academy."

A young couple on a bench nearby watched as Alice held James. "I love you, flyboy," Alice said.

James pulled back and looked at her. Now they both had tears. Then he kissed her. "I love you too."

Alice became the most precious soul he had ever known. She believed in peace and kindness, and honesty. They were together every day for six months. James was happy and close to graduating. He had found the girl with whom he would spend the rest of his life. They were in love.

While in the gym with Tabor playing basketball, Miles found them. Miles, James' cousin, also a student at the university, appeared shaken. "Miles, old buddy, what's happening?" James asked.

"Follow me, James, please."

James followed Miles outside. Something was wrong. Tabor saw them leaving and headed their way from the far end of the court.

As the cousins stood in the shade of a sagging Canyon Maple tree, Miles began, "There was a robbery at Trolley Square today. There was shooting—a stray bullet hit Alice," Miles whispered.

"Where is she?" James yelled.

Miles gripped James' head with both hands. "She died, James."

James fell to his knees and pleaded with his cousin, "Please, Miles, tell me this can't be happening."

When Tabor found them, Miles explained again.

Tabor kneeled with James and held him.

"Juni!" James gasped. "Can you bring her back?"

James had a mental breakdown that day. Pretending that Alice had left for her home somewhere in Texas, he did not attend the funeral, unable to talk about her, unable to cry. In his mind, Alice remained happy somewhere. Their romantic time together had never happened. James did the only thing he could; he blocked his human memory of her.

Ten years later, the aliens found James skiing solo at Snowbird. As he relaxed, floating up the mountain on a sun-painted chairlift, he noticed a young girl below in the shadow of a large pine tree waving up at him. "Hey, flyboy! I miss you!"

Sitting up in astonishment, he made eye contact with Alice. "Wait there! I'll be right down."

James tried to keep her in sight as long as he could. Sliding from the off-ramp, he flew down the mountain with reckless abandon. When he reached the place where Alice had magically appeared, she was gone. James collapsed on the snow, calling her name. His heart filled with wonder. Then he understood, and finally, he could cry. At last, James accepted the truth about her death. "Thank you, Juni," James said as his tears fell on the snow.

The aliens had beamed a perfect replication of Alice. Since his birth, the visitors had maintained a continuous record of James' life on Earth. The extraterrestrial craft hovered in orbit, cloaked with technology well beyond human detection. Earth's last hope had hope again.

Chapter 8

Graduation

After graduating from the University of Utah with a degree in Computer Science, James accepted a job in Salt Lake City working for EDP, a credit union service bureau. Although a rather average job, it had advantages. The company shared a large IBM mainframe with ZCMI, a popular retail store. EDP needed a Systems Engineer, and that engineer would have exclusive access to the mainframe at night.

Each evening, James would gather the punched computer cards from the girls working in keypunch and carry them to the computer room at the top of a large downtown Salt Lake City building. The girls appreciated his help and liked flirting with him. James became curious about the need to put all the day's data on punched cards. He knew there must be a better solution.

One night, while carrying two large trays of computer cards across the top of the open-air parking garage, James tripped. It was a spectacular disaster. As he stumbled, he watched all the cards flutter off the building and across the Salt Lake valley. From twenty stories up, the cards took flight. Instead of panicking, he leaned against a solid cement beam and laughed. *It was a good job while it lasted*, he thought.

After heading back to EDP and sitting in the company president's office, he prepared himself for the ax. The young president, a former IBM employee whose father founded EDP, walked in and patted James on the shoulder. "It looks like we will need to reenter today's data. That must have been something to see."

"Yeah, sorry, boss. I'm a klutz. Who would have thought those cards could fly so far?"

"It's okay, son. The girls appreciate your help, and accidents happen. Don't worry. I'll take it out of your next six months' pay."

Paul, the president, watched James' reaction in amusement. "Just kidding, James."

"Thanks, Paul. I guess I'll get back to work. It's nice to have a job still."

James got up to leave, and then he sat back down. "What if we didn't need to use punched cards?" James asked.

"What do you mean?"

"I could write software so the girls could enter their data on 3270 computer terminals remotely connected to the mainframe downtown. There would be no need for cards. If the girls made mistakes, they could edit online without entering the entire card again. And I wouldn't be hauling those unrighteous trays of cards to the top of the skyscraper."

'You can do that?" Paul asked.

"Yes, I'm sure I can," James said.

"Let's do it! Get me all the specs, and the job is yours."

James found a related two-week IBM class in Chicago. EDP paid for the course and bought his airplane tickets. Two days later, he boarded the plane, hoping to find a seat away from the smoking section. A smoking and non-smoking division made little difference, though, as smoke quickly filled the passenger cabin after takeoff.

He entered the fancy IBM building the next day and found his class. Like the airplanes, the classrooms had a smoking section on one side and non-smoking on the other. He arrived early enough to get a seat on the far side of the non-smoking area. Several women were wearing masks to help with the smoke. James wondered why they didn't have smoking and non-smoking classes in separate rooms.

The excellent teacher gave James the information necessary to write the new online system for EDP. Eager to start, James began coding his project during the course. After leaving the IBM class one night, he explored Chicago. It had a fantastic museum and several art galleries. He also visited the famous Adler Planetarium. He found a nearby movie theater and watched a new movie called *Star Wars*. James loved the movie. The theater had plenty of empty seats, but long lines packed every seat a week later.

One night, James went out looking for a sandwich and something to drink. He saw what looked like a good place, so he entered the building and jogged down the steps to the basement hangout. He sat at the bar on a stool and spun around a couple of times until a pretty girl approached him. "Hi there, handsome; what can I get you?" the friendly bartender asked.

"Could I get a lemonade and one of those grilled cheese specials on wheat?"

"Anything extra in that lemonade?"

"No, just lemonade, please," James replied.

The girl came back, and they talked for a while. As she leaned on the bar with her elbows, she noticed James looking at her breasts. She tapped him on the hand and left.

While waiting, James glanced around the room of mostly men. A young man came over and sat next to him. With a big smile, he sat looking at James but said nothing.

"What's up?" James asked.

"Meet me in the men's room, and I'll show you."

James turned away and ignored him.

After another futile attempt to get James' attention, the young man stormed off.

The girl bartender returned, looked at James maternally, and said, "This is a gay bar."

James thanked her with a wink, placed a $20 bill on the counter, and left. He ran up the stairs to leave as two men entered. "Don't go in there! It's a gay bar!" James warned.

The men laughed and continued down the stairs. James felt foolish. *Well, I'm a naïve idiot,* he thought.

He walked the noisy streets of Chicago until he found a small corner cafe and grabbed some food. He explored the city until late at night, then headed back. When he entered a dark, short-cut alley near the hotel, two men with guns approached, demanding his wallet.

James could not afford to hand over what he had, so he ignored them and kept walking. He glanced back to see a flash of gunfire as a strange glow covered his body, and the bullets fell to the ground. The eerie light and angry face startled the men, and they ran away. As he turned back, Juni appeared. "You should be more careful, James Ripley. Earth is a dangerous and primitive planet."

"What happened?" James asked.

"I surrounded you with a force field to block the deadly bullets. Are you alright?"

"Yes, I'm fine. Thanks for saving me from those jerks. But why are you here? Why didn't you save Alice?"

"You deserve answers, James Ripley. You are more than an observer; you are a creature of two worlds. You are not entirely human. You are the son of Charles and Betty Ripley, but you are also of a distant world, many light-years away. As I have explained before, you are an observer. You are the constant eyes for your other world here on Earth."

"What?! What do you really want from me?"

"Not much. We have no intention of interfering with this planet," Juni responded.

"But why is that? That is a stupid policy. You could have saved Alice."

"Because you are not entirely human, we could intervene and save you. But Earth is doomed," Juni said without emotion. "Yet fear not; we will escort you from the planet before its destruction."

"Are you going to destroy the Earth? Be honest with me."

"No, of course not. Again, we are merely observers. There are more planets in this galaxy with life forms than you might suspect. We are recording the history and end of this planet. That is all I can tell you for now. Have a good night, James Ripley. We will meet again."

You are not entirely human. Juni is crazy. James staggered back to his room and fell asleep on the bed without removing his clothes. He overslept, becoming late for class. Wanting to believe the previous night had been a dream, he showered, shaved, and ran for the IBM building.

James returned to Salt Lake three days later. If what Juni said might be true, that would change his life forever. *But so what if he was not entirely human?* James had to know why Earth was in danger.

Chapter 9

California

James built the EDP online system and then decided to move to California. He hit the road with no job offer and drove directly to a recruitment office in North Hollywood. While in the front waiting room, a young, well-dressed lady approached and sat next to him. "Hello, my name is Marsha. We have an offer for you as a model and possible actor."

"Oh, you must have me confused with someone else," James said.

"No, I have your resume here with your photograph. We have a position for you starting tomorrow if I confirm that you match your headshot."

"Well, that sounds interesting, but I'm a programmer with a computer science degree. Do you have any good prospects for a coder?"

"My associate, Mr. Wilson, will meet with you. But this modeling position is an excellent offer. There are dozens of young men fighting for this job, but they want you," Marsha explained.

"From my photograph? I have no qualifications as a model or actor."

A man approached. "Are you trying to steal my recruit, Marsha?"

"You can't blame a girl for trying. James, this is Mr. Wilson. He will help you. I enjoyed our short chat." Marsha smiled and handed James her card.

Mr. Wilson helped James secure a job offer with Home Savings and Loan. *The modeling work might have been more interesting*. James considered but then accepted the programming position.

His new gig paid better than EDP, but his first paycheck would not come for two weeks, and James had no savings. Luckily for James, his Aunt Beanie lived in San Fernando Valley. He drove his car to visit her, and she immediately offered him a large bag of carrots. His loving aunt guessed that James needed food. "They say that a person can live on nothing but carrots for weeks," said Aunt Beanie.

James did live on those carrots for almost two weeks. He resisted the temptation to sneak into a field of apple trees. He rode his bicycle to work daily to save the gas left in his car. He slept in that car and showered at a park in North Hollywood. Although James believed that his ruffled clothes were not noticeable, a secretary invited him to her place for dinner. "Bring your clothes, and I'll wash and iron them for you," she said.

"I'm that obvious?" James asked.

Nancy smiled. "I'm guessing you must be waiting for your first paycheck. I was in the same boat once myself."

Starving, the meal was fantastic. James thanked her repeatedly and hugged Nancy, his first real friend in California.

The work at Home Savings bored James. Programmers could submit a few punch cards of software code each day. He soon determined that the large company's online technology fell far behind the little EDP in Utah. James understood the improvements they needed to become current. Perhaps this company needed him.

A semi-annual chess contest for the 200+ employees had signs posted predominantly on the cork boards. Anyone could enter, and the prize boasted a whopping $100. James' boss, Roger, the current three-time champion, encouraged him to join the tournament, perhaps to humiliate him and claim his rightful position as boss.

"I don't play chess," James explained. "I have read about Bobby Fisher's strategies for beating the Russians, though."

"Do you know the moves in Chess?" Roger asked.

"Well, I played with a friend in high school. But I don't think we were any good."

"Perfect! Enter for fun. There's free food and drinks."

"Okay, why not," James replied.

James slowly defeated the halfhearted employees forced to play. To his amazement, James found himself in the final match against his surprised boss, Roger.

"So, James, you are better than you professed. What's your secret?" Roger asked before the match.

"Don't ask me. I got lucky, I guess. Please don't humiliate me; Nancy is watching."

Roger laughed, and the game began. As James surveyed the gathering crowd, he knew serious business was afoot. All the big bosses with offices, secretaries, and private bathrooms attended. Home Savings and Loan served most of Southern California.

According to Bobby Fisher, you get aggressive and stay that way. Never retreat. So that became the strategy James used against Roger. He followed the advice of the best chess player on the planet.

It took nearly ninety minutes before Roger toppled his king. The newbie, reluctant programmer became the Home Savings and Loan chess champion.

"If I had known you were that good, I would never have goaded you into entering," Roger said as he stood and shook James's hand.

"Thanks, Roger."

A Code Red alarm sounded three weeks later in the giant computer room. The main computer system had shut down, and it had been down for two hours. Every systems expert available joined the fight to fix the problem. Four IBM professionals were on site. James asked the chief systems analyst if he could take a look. Charlie shrugged and let him access the systems monitor, then left for the other side of the room, where a group of a dozen experts had gathered.

James had been the sole systems programmer for EDP, and James kept the EDP mainframe running. As he looked at the data storage statistics, he noticed the removable disc storage units were out of space. The complex had plenty of additional hardware, so the system should automatically use the next big spinning disc in line.

But the software was failing, and James knew what had broken because he once encountered the same issue at EDP. Before the next disc could be available for storage, a single bit needed flipping on the last disc. The application software could not recognize the next disc in line until someone corrected the problem.

James walked to the other side of the room and tried to get Charlie's attention. But Charlie, immersed in conversation with the powers that be, completely ignored him. After half an hour, the place crawled with panic as the shutdown was costing the company a fortune. James left the computer room and walked to the front desk, where his friend Nancy sat frightened. Beside her rested the microphone used to make building-wide announcements.

"I need that mic, Nancy," James said calmly.

"What? What for?"

"I know why the mainframe is down. But I'm unable to get anyone's attention."

"You're kidding me! Are you joking, James?"

"Nope, not kidding. Should we let them know?" James asked with a smile.

Nancy studied James and then giggled. "Go ahead, James. If we get fired, we get fired."

James picked up the microphone, and Nancy enabled it for all rooms in the building.

"This is James Ripley. While working on a similar system in Utah, I encountered the same problem you have experienced. The solution is pretty simple. A single bit in disc 14 needs flipping before the next disc is available. Currently, fourteen of your storage units are full, and the system needs more storage. I can show any of the computer room operators exactly how to fix the Code Red." Click.

James and Nancy sat at the big front desk as a herd of people ran up the hall toward them. They escorted James back to the computer room. Ten minutes later, the Code Red lights went off.

James became the company hero for a while. He had a large clean office and plenty of free time to do whatever he wanted. His programming assignments took less than an hour each day. So, James quit his tedious job as a computer programmer for Home Savings and Loan. Of course, they tried to convince him to stay, but the monotony forced him to leave. He got in his car and headed for Newport Beach. He needed some surf and sun and a job closer to the ocean.

He found an apartment complex named South Pointe less than two miles from the beach. The apartment came with tennis courts, swimming pools, and a gym. A friendly sales manager named Tammy offered him what she called a great deal. He had enough savings to make a deposit, so he moved in. A week later, the now-famous programmer landed a job working for Hydril, a pipeline monitoring company in Anaheim. His thumbs-up reference from Home Savings helped. His good-natured chess opponent came through for him.

Hydril had PIGS (big round blobs) that traveled the pipelines. But these PIGS needed software to control them. The live system used offline PIGS that offloaded data after traveling the pipes and returning. They had no online monitoring. Now, this could be a challenge because the software and the monitoring hardware did not exist.

One day after work, James met Nancy at a small club in San Jacinto. She came with a vocal group of friends. She eagerly introduced James as they gathered at the dining table. The friends told James about an organization they belonged to called Scientology. After dinner, they invited James back to their office for an evaluation. Curious, James followed them to a destiny at the mysterious headquarters.

Nancy looked excited as they strapped a device to James' arm and began their questioning. A graceful girl in a fluffy blue dress joined in the excitement. Sara, one of the managers or auditors, became interested in James, and Nancy moved her chair closer to her friend.

Sara paused the questioning and provided James with a few basic rules that he had to agree to before continuing:

• One does not disagree with anything Mr. Hubbard has said or question the authority of the Church organization.

• Scientology is beneficial and ethical, which is not open to question or discussion.

• Past life or any other knowledge obtained through Scientology's exclusive methods is normal, acceptable, and factually valid.

James quickly understood that they sought to invalidate any competing or non-supportive realm of thought that did not jive with this new church.

"Okay, sure," James said. I have no reason to question your rules. But what do you mean by past life?

Sara explained that if he matured worthy, he would eventually remember his past lives and even have the power to leave his body and travel free.

"Wow, that is impressive," James said.

Sara had a blank stare. "To begin, we need to test your emotions. That is the purpose of this device. The device on your arm is our emotion detector."

James examined the device. "This is common hardware. You have a slightly altered Wheatstone Bridge connected to my arm. This measures resistance, not emotions."

A wave of irrational anger flashed across Sara's face.

Yikes!

After she gave James her verbal reprimand, James calmly asked what the emotion detector thought about her outburst.

They abruptly escorted James from the building. He never saw Nancy again, but for almost two weeks, Sara stalked him. She sat on the beach, watching him as he jogged past. She sat in her car, observing him as he left work. She followed him to Ralphs Supermarket. Then one day, as he pulled into the parking garage and drove up the ramp, he saw her in the mirror floating behind his car with nothing but blue sky behind her. James slammed his brakes, jumped from his car, and spun around but could no longer see her.

Where's Juni when I need her? He wondered if he might be dealing with another alien life form. Perhaps more than one visitor had plans for Earth. Or maybe there was more to this mysterious Scientology than he thought. Or conceivably, a trick projection of some kind to frighten unworthy members into behaving themselves.

That ended Sara's stalking, so now James could focus on his new project. His boss at Hydril was a tall bearded fellow with narcissistic tendencies named Michael. Michael thought highly of himself. Hydril had hired Michael two months before Michael hired James. Along with James, Michael brought onboard a team of consultants. They were not employees, only highly paid computer consultants.

It became evident that neither Michael nor the consultants knew how to build the software for the new PIGS. James spent most of his time with the engineers assembling the new device. The machine came with an operating system, but the only way to program the device was in Assembly Language. No high-level languages like COBOL were as yet available from Micro Instrumentation and Telemetry Systems (MITS). The device had not been released to the public yet. So, James studied the only programming manual available. It took a few days before he could write simple instructions, but feeding the device with the instructions turned out to be a devil of a task. The machine accepted instructions by toggling bits on the portable console.

"You have to be kidding," Michael yelled when James explained.

"There is no programming input device," James said. "I have to convert the assembly code to its associated binary values and toggle it in from the console. Do you know if they plan to provide a better way to load the computer's memory? We need a stored program for these to go out with the PIGS."

Michael got back to James that afternoon. "A card reader is coming in three weeks, and a storage tape deck in two months. In the meantime, keep testing and coding. Our consultants will know what to do then." But James knew the consultants were collecting compensation for basically nothing.

James became friends with the engineering manager and the engineer assigned to building the new "brain," as he called it, for the PIGS. They added sensors and switches the brain could monitor and control with software. James and the engineers tested code snippets daily to ensure they synced with the device. James seldom talked to his boss, who spent most of his time with his consultants.

Finally, a lunch meeting, as Michael, James, and the three consultants met in Santa Monica. After an enlightening discussion, Michael decided to take a two-week class in Albuquerque, New Mexico, even though he had no computer programing experience.

The following two weeks were fun. James and the engineers made a good team. A working program controlled most of the devices needed for the PIGS. The communications network was the most difficult, but they were making progress. Still, James knew they had a primitive system.

Each day, after work, James felt lonely. The front desk secretary at Hydril flirted with him, but she had a boyfriend. James liked to play tennis and swim at his fancy resort complex in Newport, but his friends were men. Late one night, as he sat in the outdoor Jacuzzi, a gorgeous girl in a white swimsuit came to join him. They were alone, and the lights were dim as she slipped into the water on the other side. James finally recognized her as the agent from the front office who sold him his apartment. He'd thought she looked cute then, but Tammy was stunning in her swimwear.

"Hi, James," she said. "Do you remember me?"

"Sure, Tammy, right?"

Presently, Tammy glided over to his side. "It's easier to hear now," she whispered into his ear.

They chatted for a few minutes, and then Tammy moved closer and put her hand on his thigh under the water. James became aroused. She smiled and moved her hand onto his erection. Eventually, James lifted her light, seemingly ethereal, body up and onto the side of the Jacuzzi. Then he helped her remove her suit.

They were still alone. James seldom saw anyone this late at night under the palm tree, so he felt at ease. He released his trunks into the water and lifted them onto the tile. As they kissed, he slid into her. James found it surprisingly easy and smooth.

"They must use slippery soap in this tub," he said to Tammy as she grabbed the back of his head.

"Don't talk," she pleaded.

They made euphoric love for half an hour. Near the end, Tammy screamed, and James saw lights coming on in the nearby apartments. As they dressed, one of the building managers walked toward them from across the tennis courts. "Oh, hi, Tammy. Everything all right here?" he asked.

"Yes, Sam, this is James. He lives in 215. He was telling me a funny joke."

James nodded and almost burst out laughing at the quintessence of a terrible explanation. The lovers were busted.

After Sam left, James and Tammy wished each other a good night. "You have no idea how much I needed that," Tammy said.

"Ditto, sweet girl," James replied.

Before returning to his apartment, James walked in his sandals to the open parking lot. He wanted to retrieve a Sci-Fi novel by Asimov. While at the Newport outdoor shopping mall earlier, James purchased the book at Barnes and Noble. Then for lunch, he found a quiet outdoor cafe. He noticed an older man sitting at the adjacent table. The man nodded as James sat down.

Instead of lunch, James ordered a blueberry ginger smoothie and opened his new book. The man held a strange manuscript on robots. Glancing up, the man smiled and asked, "Do you think androids will eventually take over the world?"

"Well, that's funny, you should ask. I'm a computer programmer," James replied. "To be honest, I don't see that happening. But I do believe we will build intelligent robots eventually."

The two men politely debated the subject for almost an hour. The kind, brilliant gentleman knew more–James believed he could be surreptitiously hiding something. Still, James could not prevent himself from showing off his knowledge of computer systems.

"Unlike humans, our intelligent robots will make decisions based solely on logic," James explained.

"That is a fascinating conclusion. But once these immortal creatures of ours reach the singularity, the point of human intelligence, don't you think they might develop emotions?"

James studied his new friend. *Something familiar about him.* Before he could respond, the man said, "That book you have, I should tell you–I wrote it."

Epiphany! James felt like an idiot. "Oh, boy, do I feel stupid," James said.

"No, I must say how much I've enjoyed our conversation. You are an unusual and curious young man," Isaac Asimov replied.

The two men eventually bid each other farewell, and James walked to his car with a giddy smile. He held his book up to the sky, delighted with his purchase and his signed autograph from the master of science fiction.

Consumed with thought and replaying his conversation with Isaac, James had left his book in his unlocked car. The book remained there; no theft today. He reached inside, grabbed it, and held it to his chest.

Then he saw her standing in the dark, watching him. She seemed more mysterious. James approached, finding himself delighted to see her again.

"Why didn't you tell your friend, Mr. Asimov, about us?" Juni asked.

"Wow, you are keeping an eye on me," James said as he thought about Tammy.

"We found Mr. Asimov to be a rather unusual human with an outstanding and curious imagination," Juni said.

"Well, that is an understatement," James replied. "I'm a bit curious myself," he continued. "What did you think about Tammy?"

"Extraordinary! She certainly attracted your attention," Juni said.

"Juni! You need to give me a certain amount of privacy!"

Juni genuinely laughed. James stepped back in shock. He assumed the aliens were devoid of emotion.

"James, you are providing excellent observations of humans. The information is of immense historical value."

"Well, one secret deserves another. What if you tell me what happens to the Earth, and I won't be angry about your spying on me with Tammy?" James said.

"Very well, James, we will answer your questions. You have earned our respect."

"Okay, for starters, how did you know Earth had intelligent life?" James asked.

"When any star's white light is cracked open into a rainbow of its infrared ultraviolet spectrum, life on any planet orbiting the star is detectable. We notice because molecules of the planet's biosphere cast a shadow on the star's spectrum. Your atomic bombs in the 1940s made it easy for us to find you," Juni explained.

"Well, that is amazing," James replied. "One more question before I get to the biggie. Are you an android or a human?"

"I am neither, James. But I am not an artificial being. Like you, I am a natural life form. Remember, you are only half-human. The other half is like me. I am a female. You might find me attractive, almost as attractive as Tammy, perhaps," Juni replied with a strange laugh or giggle.

James whistled. "Wow, so that was you at Woodstock. I feel better about all this now for some reason. Okay, now for my next question. How will Earth be destroyed?"

Juni began, "On July 25, 2020, an asteroid 130 meters across will miss the Earth by 52,000 miles or one-fifth of the Moon's distance. Humans will observe the event with curiosity. Unfortunately, close encounters with asteroids passing through the Earth-Moon space are not unusual. By 2021, your astronomers should be tracking over 20,000 asteroids, of which 10% are hazardous.

"But these are the easily known asteroids and comets threatening the Earth. The near-Earth object population doesn't make up the entire threat. Asteroids migrate into Near-Earth space from the distant Main Asteroid Belt, a well-stocked group of rocks between Mars and Jupiter. More than two million asteroids larger than half a mile in diameter populate your asteroid belt.

"Then far beyond the Main Belt is the Kuiper Belt, a vast population of icy asteroids and comets in the Neptune and Pluto vicinity. And still far beyond the Kuiper Belt, at the very edge of Earth's solar system, is the Oort Cloud, a massive icy reservoir of more than two trillion comets. In 2021, your astronomers will likely discover a giant 62-mile-wide comet from the Oort Cloud moving toward the inner solar system. This comet is unstoppable with any human technology, even in 2021. But it will pass between Saturn and Uranus in 2031 and poses no threat to Earth. But as I said, your solar system has two trillion comets.

"In 1946, we spotted a 93-mile wide comet from the Oort Cloud that *will* strike the Earth in 2035. This comet is the beast that will end all human life on Earth. Humans do not have the technology or the, how should I say, the will to stop the inevitable. We believe your astronomers will probably know the Earth is doomed by 2031, giving them four years to flounder and ultimately accept the inescapable."

"Juni, you must help us! What harm can there be to deflecting that beast?" James begged.

"No, James, we dare not. Already, Earth is an isolated threat to intelligent life in the galaxy. We will speak again, James Ripley."

Chapter 10

Peril

James devoted himself, along with the engineers, to the Hydril PIG project, and they were making good progress. The worthless outside consultants bragged unwisely about their fees. Each one making ten times James' salary, and none of them could code. Still, despite the swaggering, James felt obligated to earn his pay and complete the project.

Michael, James' MIA boss, had signed up for another class, this time in New York. The new technology demanded more education, he argued to the company execs.

And so, the Hydril automated system for monitoring pipelines depended on one programmer with limited knowledge of assembly language and a few young electrical engineers.

After work, James spent time on friendly Santa Monica Beach for some easy surfing and group workouts. Unfortunately, the ocean contained harmful debre, unlike the waters he'd surfed in Hawaii. He wondered about the strange taste, and his eyes often burned.

While paddling out to surf one evening, he noticed someone splashing frantically below the ocean end of the Santa Monica Pier. It looked as if someone might have fallen off. He caught a smooth wave toward the pier and jumped from his board in the same vicinity. He looked up and saw a woman waving and pointing to the location below her. Swimming even closer, James dove under the water.

He surfaced and looked up again. The frantic woman remained, waving and pointing. Following her guidance, James swam for ten yards and dove again. Finally, he saw a little girl underwater and not moving. James grabbed her and brought her to the surface. Screaming observers had scattered life jackets on the water, so he used two and dragged the girl to shore. A muscular lifeguard snatched the little girl and administered CPR. Soon the child began coughing and sat up.

The hysterical woman from the pier tackled James with hugs and then ran back to the child. Presently, he noticed a group of teenagers carrying a surfboard and parading in his direction. He waited, exhausted on the wet sand.

"Good job, dude!" one of them said and planted James' surfboard in the sand.

A female lifeguard asked if he needed anything. "No, I'm good. How's the little girl?" James asked.

"She's doing fine, thanks to you. It was so lucky you spotted her."

Eventually, James lifted his board and walked back to his car. Returning to his place at South Pointe, he crashed on his couch. James planned to shower and climb into bed but fell asleep on the couch. In the morning, he awoke with a headache, a nasty sinus infection, and blurred vision. After drinking some orange juice, James stumbled down the stairs and shuffled to the club steam room. After a lengthy steam and a quick shower, he returned to his apartment.

When he called in sick to Hydril, the friendly front desk secretary offered to bring him food or drinks. "I'm pretty well stocked up, but thanks, Marcy." James found an aged ginger brew in the back of the fridge and wobbled to the outdoor patio. He fell asleep once more, and when he awoke, he felt worse.

Two days later, James met with an ENT specialist, Dr. Timothy Kelley, who took X-rays and a blood sample.

"Your illness must have been coming on for some time," the doctor explained. "A sinus infection has spread to your meninges, the protective coverings around your brain and spinal cord. There is severe inflammation."

"What can we do, Doc?" James asked.

"Unfortunately, something even more serious is happening. The infection has crossed the brain barrier. There is already slight swelling of the brain. We had a similar case last month, and the young man died," the doctor said in a strangely detached voice.

"Was he a surfer by any chance?" James asked.

"Yes, he was. But this amoeba cannot survive in saltwater."

Shivering, James asked, "What are my chances?"

"Not good, son. We will do everything we can."

"I have to survive! The fate of the world depends on it," James said, quickly realizing how irrational he sounded.

"We will take you to the hospital now and start antibiotics," the doctor said.

After three days, the doctors gave him less than a one percent chance of survival. Because of increased brain swelling, the head neurologist scheduled surgery for the next day. That night in the dark, Juni came to him. "You need to leave this place right now!" she said. "We will help you, but not here."

James managed to dress and sneak out of his room. His head pounded, and he fought an out-of-body experience while sweat poured down his face. Feeling deathly ill and with blood dripping from his nose, James willed himself to keep moving down the stairwell. He walked from the hospital across a parking lot and to an isolated field. Alone in the dark, Juni waited. A soft, warm glow surrounded James and engulfed him in a feeling of pure euphoria. The pain in his head subsided. As if by magic, his entire body gradually returned to normal. Cured of the vile disease, James asked if he could hold Juni.

"I am on my ship, James. Notwithstanding, we can give my projection texture and substance. I cannot hold you, but it will feel to you as if I am," Juni said.

"Thank you, Juni. What a wonderful gift, having you by my side all these years," James said.

James held Juni for five minutes of pain-free bliss before speaking. "Where should I go now? Back to the hospital?"

"That would be best. Tell the people in white that their primitive treatment is working, and you are ready to leave."

James gave Juni one more hug, returned to his room, and slipped into his hospital gown. Surprised at how easy it was to escape and return without notice, James walked to the nurse's desk. "Hello, ma'am, I'm feeling much better now, and I would like to check out."

The nurse checked his name tag and became frantic. "You must return to bed immediately." She grabbed a wheelchair and rolled it toward him. "The doctor was planning to contact your parents tomorrow."

James jumped to the side. The nurse returned to the desk and pushed an alarm. Three men came running down the hall, followed by a young intern.

Two of the men grabbed James and forced him into the wheelchair. As one of them pushed the chair toward James' room, James leaped from the chair and walked back.

"Your treatment worked like a miracle. I want to go home now," James said.

"That is impossible, sir. You have deadly brain swelling, a devastating infection, and a high fever. We need to get you back to bed!"

"Okay, check my vitals. I feel fine. My fever is gone," James said.

The doctor checked for fever, and a nurse tested his blood pressure. The three guards stood with arms folded, blocking his way. Throwing his arms wildly, another doctor approached. They examined James for twenty minutes, made phone calls, and rechecked him.

"We cannot let you leave. Your illness is far too severe," the head doctor said.

"And yet I am no longer sick. If I tell you the secret cure, will you let me leave?" James asked.

"I would like to hear an explanation," said the intern.

"It's simple; I'm not human," James said nonchalantly. "If you don't let me leave, there will be dire consequences for the human race."

"Let him go!" said one of the guards.

"I agree," said the nurse. "He's crazy. I'm frightened."

The other two guards stepped aside, and James walked away, but before entering the elevator, he turned and waved with a scary grin, "Goodnight, humans, and thanks for your help."

A moment later, he returned with a shrug of the shoulders because he still wore the hospital gown. After dressing, he gently approached the desk. "I was kidding, of course," he said to the nurse. "I'm sorry for scaring you. Could you call me a cab?"

James noticed five messages on his answering machine, four from Dr. Kelley. He finally returned the call and apologized to the doctor for scaring the nurse, but he declined to return for another checkup. James would trust his fate to Juni before letting the "primitive" humans have another crack at him.

The other message came from his mother. Dr. Kelly had called her with his worst possible bad news. She had left a long and fearful message, her voice cracking with emotion. James called to calm her down and told her he loved her and he felt fine. James needed a trip home and promised his mom he would see her soon.

Three weeks later, James and his Hydril team had a functioning PIG with the computerized tracking system onboard. They were celebrating in the lunchroom when Michael returned.

"In my office now!" Michael said to James.

Michael slammed the door. "Sit down!"

"What's up, boss?" James asked, rather amused.

"Who told you to put the system together? Your job was to test the equipment. That's it!"

"Just trying to get this puppy built. What's wrong?" James turned toward Michael.

Seeing the look on Michael's face, James finally understood. He was doing Michael's job. Michael became upset because they were getting the system built without him and his consultants.

"You have been wasting valuable engineering resources. This system needs to be ripped apart and rebuilt." Michael swore and threw a stapler at the chalkboard.

James stood up and walked to the door. "Where do you think you are going?" Michael screamed.

Joe, the engineering manager, waited outside the door as James left. "Hey, James. We think you are doing a great job."

At that, Michael slammed his door again. James took Joe by the arm while walking away and said, "Joe, I may need you guys. I can't explain right now, but I'll be in touch."

"Are you leaving?" Joe asked. "Son, you don't need to quit. The engineering department has your back. Hell, we will hire you if we have to."

"It's okay, Joe. I need to get back to Utah. I've enjoyed working with you, and I'll call you."

As James cleaned out his desk, Michael came at him again. "I'm not through with you; now, get back in my office!"

"Michael, I no longer work here, so I'm not obligated to do what you say," James replied.

"The hell you're not. You cost this company time and resources. Now get back in my office unless you want a lawsuit."

"Okay, Michael, I can't wait to hear what you have to say now." James stood and walked back into the lion's den.

Michael proceeded to hammer at James, but James sat quietly without responding. Finally, James said, "Are we done now?"

With that, Michael left the room. James meandered through the building, saying goodbye to his associates. The friendly girl at the front desk hugged him.

The company's president emerged from his private office and approached with a shrug. "Is there anything we can do to keep you? My engineers came in and gave you high praise."

"No, sir. I've enjoyed working here, and those engineers of yours are top-notch. I'm heading back to Utah. I talked to my old boss, and they want me back. Thanks for everything."

As James left the building, he heard the president talking to the secretary. "Where's Michael? I want him out of here!"

Great decision, James thought. He wondered if they would finally stop paying those rip-off consultants.

James managed to pack up his belongings and load them into his trusty old Mercury Comet. The following day, he entered the apartment office. Tammy had been waiting at her usual desk. While saying goodbye, she gave him a long kiss. He knew those lips well enough. The others in the office stared in surprise, but she didn't seem to mind.

James paid his rent for the rest of the month and strolled to his waiting car. His California adventure had come to a low, melancholy end. The one thing he would not miss was the crowded and dangerous freeways. James slapped in a tape and spun to the Animals' *"We Gotta Get Out of this Place."* He pondered about what adventures awaited him back in Utah. He had Juni, and the terrifying fate of the entire planet, on his mind.

Chapter 11

New Language

"I've used most of IBM's programming tools, Paul, and they are too slow. Compile and test, compile and test. All the languages are the same, from Assembler to Cobol to the hybrid languages. I want to start a new company, but I need your mainframe because I don't have a million dollars for a computer," James explained.

"What is your idea this time?" Paul asked.

"Let's start a new company. I want to write a new language. We will use the credit unions as our guinea pigs, but this could end up in use everywhere."

Paul laughed. "What kind of new language? You have my attention, but this sounds crazy."

"I believe I can build a fully interpretive language," James said. "Think about it. There would be no compiling. Developers would write the code and simply run it. The engine interprets the code and runs immediately—the world's first entirely interpretive language. Programmers would go bonkers with this kind of tool."

With that, Paul sat up. He looked at James for a long time. As an IBMer, he knew about the theory of interpretive languages. "This sounds like it would take years and a team of programmers," Paul said.

"Nope. I'll write it myself in less than two years. I've been thinking about this for a long time," James said as he approached the chalkboard.

He wrote "Software Generation Technology (SGT). 51% owned by James Ripley, 49% owned by EDP."

"I know it's risky, but your expense is only my current salary and use of the mainframe. If we pull this off, it will be fun! I'll need your help with testing on the credit unions and finding a buyer, but that's what you are good at."

"So basically, you are not here to work for EDP; you want to build this thing," Paul said.

"Look, we will generate a new EDP online system written in SGT. I'll need a couple of programmers for that once SGT is ready. But you get SGT ownership and a new EDP online system."

"I need time to think about this, James," Paul said as he stood and left the room.

Meeting over? James wondered.

Thirty seconds later, Paul returned. "Okay, let's do it. I'll get Randy, our lawyer, to draft the docs and help form the new company."

And with that, SGT began. EDP now owned its Mainframe computer and no longer shared it with the ZCMI retail store. James had an office adjacent to EDP, where he worked in solitude. The jokes commenced when the word got out about James Ripley writing a new language. Bud and Tom, IBM systems engineers, stopped by often to chat and tease him. EDP's employees laughed when they walked past his office. But Paul believed in the project, and that was all that mattered.

James would run five miles a day while coding in his head. Later, he would drive to work and key in the new code on the mainframe's 3270 terminal. His parents were having financial problems, so James needed to finish SGT soon and help them pay their bills. SGT required all his physical and mental energy. "These are the times that try men's souls," he told his dad.

Fourteen months into the project, he found Paul and said, "Ready for a demo?"

"Damn right! Let's go."

The demo sailed impressively, but there remained a secret problem. The engine ran too slow, and James had not told anyone. In theory, SGT should work, but James had not yet solved the last lingering issue.

He found himself praying to God as he thought about his mom. He knew there must be a solution if he could only find it. He had read about a similar project at Stanford, where they decided to scrap the idea. Perhaps when computers were much faster, they decided, the interpretative language would make sense.

One morning, as James jogged in an isolated field, he prayed again. "Please, God, help me," he spoke out loud.

James believed in God for as long as he could remember. An alien hybrid with a belief in God. But when Alice died, he'd forgotten about God for a while. His inherent understanding of computer technology and progress in the software system he invented convinced him that an answer existed.

Programming is a creative art, not merely logic and math. James needed a unique stroke of the brush.

Stopping in front of a tree, he noticed a magpie. As the bird flew from the tree, the world slowed down. The bird floated in one place, the leaves stopped moving, and the wind stood still. James could see all the code in his mind, and suddenly he spotted it—the solution now so simple.

Later that day, James tested the mysterious code fix, and it worked! The great thing about computer software is if it works, it works.

The revolutionary new Interactive Application Development System for CICS hit the market. The friendly ad hoc query system with file and database management attracted the attention of several large companies, including Pansophic, Computer Associates, Oracle, and EDS. IBM invited James to give a talk at a software seminar in Chicago, the city now so familiar.

James began his talk, "In recent years, computer technology has improved so rapidly that memory capacity and throughput speeds are no longer the pacing items. Emphasis has shifted to the efficient generation of software.

"Application packages purchased 'off the shelf' are frequently limited in scope, difficult to modify, and expensive to maintain. The conventional development of application programs 'in-house' is costly, time-consuming, and requires a highly trained staff. Marginal improvements in programming productivity will not suffice. A revolutionary new approach to software generation is needed.

"SGT can do the job. Unlike software development tools from the age of batch computing, SGT is a completely integrated system designed for the interactive online environment. SGT performs the functions of many other software packages but reduces program development time and cost. SGT conserves your existing software and hardware resources. SGT programs are efficient at runtime...."

James remembered the miracle that made SGT efficient at runtime with a smile—his secret. After the conference, James left the noisy room and ran down the steps. As he exited the stairwell, a large man with a southern accent blocked his way.

"James, my name is David Winston. Pansophic would like to make you an offer for your software. Can we speak in private?"

"I guess so. I'm headed back to the Marriot. Do you want to meet me in the lounge?" James replied.

Later, David made a preliminary offer of $1.5 million, depending on their due diligence. James said he would consider it and agreed to another meeting in Salt Lake City the following week.

James told his parents about the offer and explained why he had no plans to accept. He wanted to travel to California and meet with Larry Ellison, Oracle's founder because SGT and the Oracle database would be a remarkable combination.

A meeting with EDS, founded by Ross Perot, had also been scheduled for the following week. James chuckled at the thought of that meeting. After graduating from the University of Utah, James interviewed with EDS for employment. He arrived with his friend Doug, another computer science graduate. Doug had left the meeting almost in tears. "That was excruciating, James. I feel worthless. Good luck. Better yet, just run!"

James stood when the secretary called his name, entered the torture chamber, and sat down. A tall man approached with stern disdain and began the interrogation. The interview lasted five minutes before the man, who never gave his name, said, "James, this is a waste of time. What happens if you can't make the mustard? From what I'm seeing, you have no chance of success in a company like EDS. So, what will you do when the charade is over?"

"Well, I'm not worried about that," James replied. "If I can't make the mustard, I'll just transfer to personnel management and take a position interviewing terrified college students for employment."

That ended the interview. James pushed open the door with a big smile to see Doug waiting. After a brief explanation and some good laughs, the two friends headed for the gym.

At the meeting in Salt Lake with Pansophic, James stood, thanked everyone, and said he needed to get back to work. For several days James continued his efforts to meet with Larry Ellison. The following week, David Winston called James to tell him that Pansophic had increased the offer to $4 million.

Wishing he could have met with Larry, James accepted the offer and agreed to work for Pansophic for one year. With the check deposited, James drove to his parent's house. He found his mother crying at the kitchen table with papers scattered *from hell to breakfast*.

"Mom! What's wrong?" James asked.

"Oh, nothing. It's these bills. Your father is still sick, and we might have to sell our house."

James approached the table and picked up several of the bills. "What are you talking about? You don't have any bills." James put his hand on his mother's shoulder and placed Pansophic's cashed check receipt on the table in front of her. "I'm paying all these stupid bills, and that motorhome dad always wanted is a done deal."

James scrambled down the stairs like a kid with one swing on the railing and gave his dad the good news. He would remember this as one of the best days of his life on Earth.

James Ripley had become an incredible programmer and a lousy businessman. Three years later, Pansophic sold SGT to Computer Associates for $700 million, and CA renamed SGT to GENER/OL. It was a business blunder, but James' precious moment with his parents replaced any regret. Besides, James was plotting the survival of planet Earth, and he had a new idea.

Chapter 12

Awakening

In 1984, the Porsche 928S traveled the same route to Area 51 that James Ripley had followed in 1969. James provided his name at each gate and said he wanted to speak with J-Rod. Although a long shot, James proceeded through the security stations until he found himself back at S-4, south of Groom Lake, the secret base.

James parked his car and hiked to the familiar hangars. He stepped into the one where he remembered meeting J-Rod. A familiar face awaited, the excited nerd who had led James to the flying saucer. "James, my name is Bob. Do you remember me?"

"Yes, I do. Thanks for meeting me. Is J-Rod still around?"

"You don't know? J-Rod became trapped inside the saucer. After you left, the entrance opened. J-Rod and some others entered. Then the gateway shut. We presume they are all dead."

"What? We need to get inside that flippin' saucer!" James said.

"We have tried. We've been trying since J-Rod got trapped. That thing is resilient! Nothing penetrates it. Do you know how to get in?" Bob asked with pleading eyes through what looked like the same spectacles from so long ago.

"No, not yet, but the survival of Earth depends on us getting that thing working. There must be a way inside. Let's go!"

"Yes! Let's go." Bob replied.

As he walked back down the slight incline, it seemed like yesterday. Nothing much had changed. But now a dozen scientists and two military soldiers accompanied him. James remembered the location of the entrance handgrip he tested years ago. Upon finding the hand impression, James reached toward the ship. There were no objections, so he settled his hand into the exotic lock.

Once again, he felt a tingling sensation, but the entrance would not open. This time James left his hand in the impression longer. He felt what seemed like a question, so he concentrated on opening the door.

Then he noticed motion, so James removed his hand. The entrance rolled up and disappeared with a smooth, silent action. Standing at the opening were J-Rod and his companions. They had not aged.

“Are you all right?” Bob yelled.

“The door closed before us and then opened. You’ve aged. How long have we been inside?” J-Rod asked.

“Fifteen years! Bob exclaimed.

“We must have been in some form of suspended stasis,” J-Rod said. “For us, it seemed like seconds. You have aged, Bob. And you as well, James. How did you re-open the starship?”

“James put his hand in the impression, and the entrance rolled open,” explained Bob.

“James, I knew you were an alien. Did you come to rescue us?” asked J-Rod.

James told Bob to ask the other scientists to leave, but the excited group had no intention of missing anything. J-Rod walked from the ship and ordered the scientists to leave. The shrugging, grumbling, and angry band of scientists finally withdrew.

"No, I've come to rescue the Earth. We need this ship," James replied.

He provided J-Rod with a short synopsis and concluded with the date of Earth's demise. "Any chance we can get this ship flying, dude?"

"What is 'dude'?" asked J-Rod.

"Just lingo. Never mind. If we get the ship running, I have a plan to stop the monster comet."

"J-Rod, you've been standing here for fifteen years! Are you hungry or anything?" Bob asked.

J-Rod ignored the question and spoke with concern. "Dude, have you thought about the consequences of saving the Earth? Juni told you why they refuse to interfere. Humans are a dangerous and violent species. Imagine turning them loose on the galaxy. Even if you stop the comet, humans will likely destroy themselves or search the stars for other planets to invade."

After an hour of debate, Bob convinced the group to leave for the lunchroom. In the café, J-Rod again asked for privacy from other scientists surrounding them. The discussion regarding the survival of the planet continued. Gradually, J-Rod persuaded James to reconsider.

"Okay, your arguments are compelling," James said. "But what if we get this starship, as you call it working just in case?

"I suspect Juni and those who built the craft will prevent that, but it's worth a try," J-Rod said.

"Well, you can be sure they will know. Juni's ship keeps a constant eye on me."

"Have you considered the possibility that Juni and the others left this ship here on purpose? What if they want you to save the Earth?" Bob asked.

Both James and J-Rod froze and stared at Bob. "That is an interesting question," said J-Rod. "But the ship crashed. There is no doubt about that."

"It crashed, but there were no injuries, no bodies, and no damage to the ship," said Bob.

"Well, they didn't leave instructions, and from what Juni has said, they are not here to help," said James.

"Perhaps they want you to decide," J-Rod continued. "If that's true, you have an imperative responsibility to determine if humanity can reach the next level of civilization before they have starships. Wars are raging across the planet. Humans are responsible for massive environmental damage."

"Okay, J-Rod, that makes sense, I guess, but now that I have a viable understanding of who I am, I'd like to ask you the same question. Are you an alien?"

"Fair question. Some people believe that I'm an insectoid human from the future. The irony is that I'm supposed to know of a future catastrophe that will destroy most life on Earth. But if your monster comet hits the Earth, there will be no life, not with a comet that large.

"I look strange, so I let them believe what they want. But I am not a partial insect, nor am I from the future. I have a CHRM2 genetic positive variation resulting in a cumulative IQ and logical reasoning enhancement. The bottom line is that I am dreadfully smart and have an oblong head," J-Rod explained.

"Would you rather be cute and stupid, or ugly and smart?" asked Bob.

"What?" J-Rod was confused.

"It's a joke. Forget about it," said James as he winked at Bob.

"I'm sorry, J-Rod. You know I'm a nerd. That hasn't changed in fifteen years," said Bob with a shrug.

"All right, so we have an alien hybrid, an oblong genius, and a comic science nerd. The Earth is in good hands," said James.

J-Rod looked confused. *For such a genius, he's kind of stupid*, James thought.

James spent two hours teaching J-Rod how to open and close the starship. The communication from hand to ship was subtle, but eventually, J-Rod mastered the lock.

"Keep working on the ship. See if she can fly. But keep the purpose quiet. Having a secret project inside a secret base should be possible. Otherwise, there could be worldwide panic."

"I agree," said J-Rod.

"But how can the Earth find a way to evolve beyond tribal aggression?" Bob asked.

"That is the question. I need more information from Juni," James said. "How do I stay in touch with you and J-Rod?"

Bob went to a nearby drawer and retrieved a small handheld device. He pressed multiple buttons and handed it to James. "Our conversations are encrypted with this technology. Press A51&4* to connect directly to us."

James bid farewell to his friends and left Area 51. Traveling north back to Salt Lake, he stopped in Cedar City, Utah, left his car, and walked toward the distant green hills with red rocks. He noticed several mountain bikers in the distance. The air smelled fresh with the scent of cedar trees and sage. He found a friendly tree stump and sat down to meditate. He took out his notepad to record his thoughts.

"Millions of humans follow leaders because of primitive tribal instincts. They reach a point where logic and truth have no purpose. The tools used for mind control include hate, cults, religion, lies, repetition, and guilt. Eventually, the leaders can do no wrong, and no sacrifice is too great for them. Humans are dangerous because of greed, ego, and the strange way a handful controls and divides the rest of them.

"Yet despite their weakness, humankind has managed to build various forms of government. Although they are easily manipulated, laws for good have evolved."

James continued to ponder. "We could not fly, so we built planes. We could not survive diseases, so we invented medicine. We could not see at night, so we managed fire and developed electric lighting. We could not do math fast enough, so we built calculators and computers. Besides our tribal instincts, there is a need for progress. It would be wrong to turn humans loose on the galaxy until they evolve beyond wars. So, what if humans could overcome delusion with enlightenment?

"Many believe that artificial intelligence will bring the end of humanity. Yet, without the next step, humans will perish on their own because of their inability to control their destiny or because they will self-destruct from their weapons of mass destruction.

"Humans need to accelerate the birth of AI. To reach the singularity, the point where machine intelligence exceeds human intelligence, I need to learn more—a lot more. I need to talk with the futurist Ray Kurzweil. He is an AI advocate and has a track record for accurate predictions.

"Kurzweil believes computers will have human-level intelligence by 2029. By 2045, we will have achieved singularity, and humans will connect their brains directly to AI. That is when things will accelerate. But Earth will be long gone by then.

"We know it is coming, but the question is: Should humanity fear the singularity? Most believe that when machines become more intelligent than human beings, they might take over the world. Stephen Hawking, Elon Musk, and even Bill Gates believe that scenario.

"Well, Kurzweil doesn't think so. He isn't worried about the singularity. He is an advocate. For Kurzweil, what science fiction depicts as the singularity—at which point a single brilliant AI enslaves humanity—is just that: fiction.

"For Kurzweil, the singularity is an opportunity for humankind to improve. He envisions the same technology that will make AIs more advanced will give humans a boost as well. And that could be the key to the evolution of human civilization."

James drafted a short letter to Kurzweil.

> *My name is James Ripley. I was born in 1947, and I've had a career in computer science since 1971. Do you have any thoughts on accelerating the singularity? This letter might seem strange, but humanity cannot wait until 2045. We need to build tools for advancing intelligence before*

2031. *The need to prevent self-destruction is obvious, but we face another threat that humanity cannot stop.*

Not expecting a reply, James sealed the letter for mailing.

On the road again and exhausted, James reminisced about his surfing days. *I'll fly to Mexico, play on the white sand beaches, and climb a pyramid. If I find romance, all the better.*

Chapter 13

Cancun Getaway

On the north of Mexico's Caribbean coastline, Cancun has beautiful white sandy shores, all-night parties, and excursion adventures. James boarded his four-hour United flight to Cancun with nothing but the science fiction novel Ringworld and a single suitcase.

With no clue what he would find, he needed a break. He finished his book before landing. Later, after checking into his room at the Cancun Caribe, he went exploring. Outside, he found two large pools, one circular and the other with an oddball shape. Walking past the pools and lounge chairs, he found the beach, a perfectly pure white sand carpet that led to the sparkling Caribbean Sea.

Smiling, James set off for a jog. A mile into his run, he noticed a rain cylinder about thirty feet wide. The isolated aberration had no rain outside of the circle. James paused beside the thing and walked in. Cancun gifted James a shower with a pristine ocean view. From inside, he spotted a curious girl watching him. James waved, and the girl laughed, waved back, and ran away.

Later that night, James followed a group of tourists to the Coco Bongo. Inside were sun-tanned kids dancing, drinking, and eating. James found a single small table and ordered Camarones embarazados. Looking up, he saw the girl from the shower aberration walking past. She glanced at him, stopped, and returned.

"You were having fun today," she said

"That was something. I couldn't resist. I could see you laughing at me from inside the funnel or whatever it was."

" My name's Maria."

"Hi, I'm James. Pleased to meet you."

"So, you look lonely, James. What are you doing in Cancun?"

"Oh, I needed a break. I've been working too much. What about you?"

"I'm with some girlfriends from New Orleans. We come here to relax. It's just a jump across the Gulf of Mexico puddle."

Maria reminded James of Wendy, his second-grade girlfriend. He almost made the tragic mistake of telling her she reminded him of a second-grader. "Would you care to join me for a lemonade?" James asked.

"I could tell you don't drink. Two sober people in an all-night club in Cancun." Maria pulled up a chair and sat down.

"This is an all-night club? What do we do?" James asked.

"We dance! Come on, let's go," Maria said as she pulled James by the hand and led him to one of the dance floors.

After three hours of dancing, drinking lemonade, and talking, they walked outside into the soft, warm air and toward the beach. "Do you know of any sites I should visit while I'm here?" James asked.

"Yes! You should visit the Chichen Itza Pyramid. It's about a two-hour drive. What time should we go?" Maria asked.

"You would take me? That's fantastic. I'll get us a car tomorrow. What if we leave around 10 am?"

"Perfect! You will love this place. There are ninety-two steps to the top. Want to see if we can run up it?"

"I'm game. Should I walk you back to your room?" James asked.

"No, I'm with my friends. They're still inside. I'm staying at the Cancun Caribe. Can you pick me up there at ten?"

"That will be easy. That's my hotel. Let's meet by the circular pool, and I'll have a car reserved."

Maria headed toward the club, paused, and ran back and hugged him. "Thanks for not hitting on me. Can I bring a friend with us tomorrow?"

"Of course. The more, the merrier," James said.

Maria found James in the lobby looking at a large map while talking to the hotel's attractive female concierge. James turned and gave Maria a hug.

"My friend decided not to join us," Maria said, "she is pretty hung over. Are you ready?"

"That I am, and I'm excited." James thanked the concierge and took Maria to the rental car he had waiting for them.

On the two-hour drive, and they encountered native Mayans at each rest stop. The Mayans were generally short, chubby, friendly, and eager to sell food and Coca-Cola. Upon reaching the Itza Pyramid, or Kukulcán, Maria raced James to the steps and began her count down—then they were off. She ran surprisingly fast but faded a little near the end. James slowed with her as they reached the top in a tie.

"You waited for me on purpose," Maria gasped. "So now add chivalry to your list of surprising qualities."

Standing outside the top chamber entrance, the site was spectacular. "What is that serpent for?" James asked.

"Oh, the plumed serpent is symbolic of Quetzalcóatl, known to the Maya as Kukulcán. He's one of the major deities of the ancient Mesoamerican pantheon."

"I've heard of Quetzalcoatl," James replied.

"Actually, this pyramid was built over a preexisting temple," Maria said. "The Spanish conquistadors called it El Castillo. These ruins are evidence of a stunning ancient city once the center of the Maya empire that stretched over all of Central America."

"Wow, you know this stuff. What do you do for a living, Maria?"

"I'm a high school teacher. I teach history. Were you a good boy in school, James?"

James laughed. "Not exactly. I barely graduated. I spent a lot of my high school days in the hall."

"What do you do now? You have confidence and intelligence to go along with those good looks." A breeze ruffled Maria's hair, and a ray of sunlight lit up one side of her face.

Damn, she is gorgeous, James thought.

"Oh, sorry, I was distracted by my beautiful companion. What did you ask?"

Maria moved closer and stroked his dark hair. "I was asking what you do for a living."

"I'm a computer programmer. I managed to graduate from the University of Utah with a degree in Computer Science."

"I've never been kissed by anyone at the top of a pyramid before. Are you going to kiss me, James?" Maria put her hands on her hips.

Déjà vu. James tried thinking of an excuse. Finally, he decided the truth would be more interesting, and Maria remained standing with her hands on her hips.

"Well, when I was in the second grade, a girl asked me that same question. I wanted to kiss her, but I was afraid, and I pleaded with her to run so I could chase her."

Maria laughed. "I know, James. I had no problem recognizing you, and I still love you chasing me. My name is Wendy Maria Patterson. I grew up in Utah. We went to East Millcreek elementary school together."

"Are you kidding me!? I wanted to tell you last night that you reminded me of Wendy. But telling a lady they remind you of a second grader would be crazy. I cannot believe this. What are the odds?"

"I still have a crush on you, James, and I'm still waiting for an answer."

"Ok, run down the pyramid, and I'll try to catch you," James teased as he pulled her close and kissed her.

"That was worth the wait, James. Kiss me again."

Driving back to Cancun, their car broke down. "This is not a good place to be alone in the dark, James. We need to find a way back. We can't stay here in the car."

James popped the hood and jumped out. Wendy found a flashlight in the glove box and brought it to him. "I'm no mechanic," James said. "The car's not overheated, and our gauge says we have gas. If I remember, the nearest town is about five miles."

"Let me try to start it while you watch," Wendy said.

"Okay, good idea. I'm ready. Give it a crank."

"See anything?"

"No, the starter cranks the engine, but I can't see anything."

Two men pulled up in a noisy black pickup. They got out and walked toward the rental car. "Having problems?" the taller one asked.

"Our car stopped. No idea what's wrong," James replied.

The other man walked close to Wendy and stared at her for too long, so she moved to James' side. "Don't be afraid, sweetie," the man said as he followed her.

"You guys sound American. Where are you from?" James asked as he grabbed Wendy's hand.

"New Orleans. Hop on in, and we will give you a ride for $200 or some fun with your lady friend."

"Now, Jake, that's no way to treat these people. Just get the guy's wallet, and we will be on our way," said the bigger of the two.

"Oh, shit!" Wendy said as she clung to James' arm.

"I had a couple clowns try to rob me in Chicago. It did not go well for them." When James smiled, it startled the little thief, Jake.

James felt Wendy shaking, and that pissed him off. "Get in your truck and hit the road, assholes!" James yelled.

The larger asshole ran for their truck and pulled out a gun. But as he turned, another car approached, with its headlights on high, and stopped. The man put the gun back on the seat of the truck.

A beautiful lady left the car and walked toward them. James recognized her immediately.

"Does anyone need a cab?" Juni asked.

James burst out laughing, and Wendy spun toward him in surprise.

"Gentlemen, my ride is here; now, get lost."

The tall jerk reached back for his now missing gun. With that, both thieves desperately climbed into their truck and left.

"Yes, ma'am, we need a ride back to Cancun. That was perfect timing. Those two hoods were attempting a stickup."

"Oh, my!" said Juni. "Well, get in, and I'll take you back."

"How much will it cost?" James couldn't help himself.

"What? I'll pay for it!" exclaimed Wendy.

"You can't afford me, so no charge this time," Juni said with a smile.

Alien humor, James thought.

They gathered their belongings, locked the broken rental, and climbed into Juni's mysterious cab.

"This car looks new," James said. "Do you rescue people in distress often?"

"Not often, at least not here," said Juni. "But we make good money at Galactic Cab, driving tourists to the ruins."

"Galactic Cab, that's some name."

"Do you two know each other?" Wendy finally asked.

After a long silence, James said, "We do indeed. I met Juni at Woodstock in 1969. How have you been, Juni?"

"Fine, sir. I do remember you now. Is your name James, by any chance?"

"Good memory, Juni."

Exhausted, Wendy snuggled up to James and finally stopped shaking. The ride back ended uneventfully as Juni dropped them off at their hotel.

Before entering the large doors, James walked back to the cab and leaned on the door. "Thanks again, Juni. That could have ended badly."

"You are welcome, James. Those two are killers. We had to act." The alien smiled as she drove away.

Once inside the hotel, Wendy asked James if she could stay with him. "My room is crowded with girls, and I'm still scared."

"Of course, Wendy. That was a bad situation."

"I'm wondering, why were you so brave? Do you have defense skills or something?" Wendy asked.

"Not really. I'm kind of a wimp, normally. But they reminded me of Sammy, and that was too much."

"Oh, yeah, Sammy, the bully. How did you remember his name?"

"I guess I never forgot it. But we were blessed today with that guardian angel from Galactic Cab."

Once in bed, Wendy snuggled close again. She stirred up emotions James had not felt in a long time. *She is irresistible.*

They made love twice that night and, in the morning, went for a long run on the soft sand beach. James returned first, looked to the sky, and shouted, "I think you want me to save this planet, Juni!"

As Wendy finished her run, she heard him but asked no questions.

Chapter 14

Waterfall Miracle

Wendy loved visiting James in Salt Lake, and her parents still lived there. James bought a house in Olympus Cove on the mountain's edge, four miles from his parents.

"James, we landed. I'm headed for luggage."

"Okay, I'm here now. That was perfect timing."

Wendy came down the escalator at the Salt Lake airport with a broad smile and waving arms. *I'm able to love again*, James thought as he waved back. Talking about Alice was still painful, so he'd never told Wendy. Perhaps he never would.

They left the airport, drove to I-215, then up to Wasatch Blvd on the East Bench, traveled past

James' parent's and Skyline High, and finally up Jupiter Drive to James' home. Wendy ran directly to the outdoor patio with its spectacular view of the Salt Lake City valley.

James' black lab, Data, found her and attacked. They wrestled for a while and finally settled on a soft lounge chair together. "I love you too, Data," Wendy said as she rubbed his ears.

Wendy called her mom to let her know she had arrived safely. Later they made passionate love on the outdoor patio. Wendy screamed so the neighborhood knew she had returned.

The next day after a long hike in the mountains, James followed Data into the backyard to find his tiger toy that had dropped from the porch while playing with Wendy. He noticed a black cable running from an outlet on the south side of his house to his neighbor's home, the Patels'.

James walked to the neighbor's front door and rang the bell to tell them he would be calling the police. A young boy answered. "Are your parents home?" James asked.

"My mom left us because my dad lost his job. He's downstairs crying again," the boy said without emotion.

Well, that was TMI, James thought. "Could I talk with him?"

"Okay, follow me."

James found his neighbor, Andrew, in his downstairs office at his desk. "Hello, neighbor," James said.

"Oh, hello, James. How are you doing?" Andrew came to the US from India twenty years ago but still had a bit of an accent.

"I'm fine. Sorry to hear about Darla. Are you okay?"

The other two boys entered the room. They all seemed subdued, not their usual playful selves.

"Yes, Darla found someone else and moved to California. It is my fault for losing my job with Motor Cargo. It was a good job, but the CEO is a jerk. I got tired of him yelling at me, and I told him to stop."

"Damn, that is harsh, dude. What can I do to help?"

"We have been using your electricity for two weeks. I wanted to tell you, but I was too embarrassed. I had no money to pay the power bill because Darla emptied our bank account before she left. They pull the plug fast around here."

"That's why I stopped by. I saw the cable. I was tempted to call the police."

"Please, Mr. Ripley, don't tell on my dad," said the oldest of the three boys.

"I won't, Josh. I don't want you kids to worry."

James sat down with Andrew to get an understanding of his financials. Without his job, he could no longer make house payments or cover utilities and food. James told him he would cover all those costs until he was back on his feet with a new job.

"I promise I will pay you back, James. I don't know what to say. You are the best neighbor anyone could have." All four surrounded James and hugged him.

James had loaned money to others before without reimbursement, so he didn't expect much, and he felt okay with that.

He went home, and he told Wendy about his neighbor's troubles. "You are such a good guy, James. Most people would have called the police and filed a lawsuit. I love you." Wendy kissed James and Data barked with jealousy.

The Patels moved out four months later, so James quit making their house payments. He had no idea where they had gone. But five months later, on

Christmas Eve, the doorbell rang, and Andrew stood at the door with a smile and a check.

"Yes, of course, I will marry you," Wendy said as her eyes watered.

"That went better than I thought it would," James replied. "Are you willing to leave New Orleans?"

"Yes, silly. Skyline needs teachers, and I've missed Utah. But where's my ring?"

"Oh, dumb. I've never done this before. Here it is." James got to one knee, pulled the engagement ring case from his shirt pocket, dropped it, picked it back up, extracted the ring, and slid it onto Wendy's finger.

"Okay, let's finish our hike now that we have that scary part done," said James.

"Still afraid of me? My mom is going to love this. She told me in the second grade that you wanted to kiss me but were afraid."

"She was right. You have a smart mom."

The intermediate hike up Belle Canyon began the short climb to the pristine reservoir from the parking lot on 9400 South. Next, they hiked a more advanced trail to the waterfall.

"Let's check out the top of that beast," James said.

"Okay. I think we follow this same trail up and then take a left to where the waterfall is," said Wendy.

They reached a grove with a small winding river that led to the top of the waterfall, so they followed the stream. Near the rushing waterfall, the stream narrowed and sped up. They hopped across the stream and proceeded down. When within 200 feet of the waterfall, Wendy dropped her backpack. James bent down to pick it up just as Wendy turned.

She knocked James into the rapid stream, and he grabbed her left leg. Wendy latched onto a tree limb but could not maintain her grip. James saw her hand sliding down the branch and let her loose before he pulled her in with him.

"James!" Wendy screamed.

Flying down the rapids toward the top of the waterfall and over the cliff, he struggled desperately to escape, but the side of the river had nothing but slippery moss.

I need to do something. Another thirty feet and I'm a goner. He pulled both feet up to the river's moss-covered embankment and pushed off. Diving to the other side, his hands groped the familiar slippery moss again. This time his right forefinger felt a small protruding pebble of a rock, and that was enough. One finger on a tiny stone saved his life. While clinging to the tough little gem, the current swept his feet up from the river, and James scrambled to freedom a mere ten feet from going off the Belle Canyon waterfall with nothing but giant boulders at the bottom.

Rolling onto his back, he rested, giving thanks to the gods of the universe. Standing, he worked his way back up the side of the deadly stream until he saw Wendy lying on the ground, crying.

"Wendy," he yelled, and she jumped up.

When he reached her, she clung to him with super strength. "I saw you go over the waterfall! How did you survive?"

"It was close. With ten feet left, I managed to get out of the river. One single pebble poking up in the damn moss saved me."

"I can't believe it. I thought you were gone. Gone on the very day you asked me to marry you. Oh, James, I love you beyond words. Don't ever leave me."

The couple carefully headed back down the trail to their car and drove home.

Where was Juni when I needed her that time? James wondered.

"We almost lost our observer," Juni reported. "It happened too fast for us to act, but James survived. He survived against all odds. We may have underestimated him."

Chapter 15

Mount Olympus

"Do you remember the Soviet naval officer who saved the world on October 27, 1962?"

"What? Sorry, Wendy, this AI research is consuming," said James.

Wendy continued, "Thank you for finally sharing with me what you are going through. I love you, and this is frightening. I was thinking about the sailor who refused to fire a nuclear missile and saved the world from World War III and the end of human life on Earth. Humans can rebel against the insanity of self-annihilation. Vasili Arkhipov proved that by refusing to follow his captain's orders."

"You know so much about history. I vaguely remember reading about that. That was a close call."

"I thought his story might help you. One man made all the difference during the Cuban Missile Crisis. The nuclear torpedo on his submarine could only be fired if the captain and the political officer agreed. Each had half of a key that unlocked the firing mechanism when joined. The captain wanted to fire, but Vasili refused. So don't give up on Earth, James. One person can make a difference."

James stood and gave Wendy a long hug. More relaxed, he returned to his research, looking for a way to convince the aliens that Earth was worth saving.

Scientists, educators, and politicians have spread fears among the public about the risk of AI starting a nuclear conflict. Policymakers and global defense communities warn about artificial intelligence and its military capabilities, particularly in the nuclear sphere. James knew the misconceptions were primarily caused by the hyperbolic depictions of AI in popular culture and science fiction disaster movies.

Humanities critical analysis needed to shift to the positive. AI can help manage operational, tactical, and strategic decisions far better than humans alone. Examples are everywhere, including disease diagnosis and treatment. AI could be fundamental to making the Earth safe from nuclear disasters.

James opened his laptop and began the first draft of his letter to the aliens.

> *If nuclear powers believe they can leverage AI to achieve a first-mover advantage, AI will destabilize the fragile deterrence of mutually assured destruction. But if all nuclear parties come together for their combined benefit by taking steps toward establishing a common AI governance system that controls the deployment of nuclear weapons, accidental or first-strike war will cease. And that is the first step toward intelligent and safe worldwide nuclear weapons disarmament...*

Sixteen hours later, James sent his futile letter to Juni, pleading with the aliens to help stop the comet.

Chapter 16

Unacceptable

James received the response from the aliens and eagerly translated the encrypted message.

Since the day you were born on Earth, we have studied the human inhabitants. The fate of any race depends on its ability to end self-deception. As a perspicacious observer, you know that world leaders lie to the multitudes. How will humanity advance beyond *self-delusion when so many are easily misled by so few?*

You make an interesting argument for the positive influence of artificial intelligence in advancing human knowledge, integrity, coherence, and disarmament. But do you believe there is time? Humans have not yet achieved singularity.

As for now, a warmongering race controls the Earth. And the senseless wars are almost always based on disinformation. The leaders lie to start wars because the wars benefit only the oligarchs. The few humans seeking the truth become chastised and ignored. Yet, we find humanity itself is unstable.

Network information outlets could help, but they fear weaponized feedback. They are complicit in disinformation while advancing impossible narratives.

There is a long history on Earth of false flags and disinformation. Logical reasoning depends on the population rejecting deceitful fabrications, but humans are programmed, almost at birth, to avoid conflict with authority. The damage is inherited and pervasive throughout the human species, like a bad gene.

Humans find themselves on a planet with nuclear weapons pointed at each other. Wars between countries rage, not for freedom, but for the profit of the greedy few in charge. Humanity has been destroying the planet's environment for decades. They seem to delight in self-destruction.

A pandemic strikes the Earth, and the people rebel against science as if eliminating the virus is an as-

sault on their freedoms. They accept false narratives. But their delusions should serve them well as the comet approaches because they will easily deny it is coming. Forgive me for that insensitive comment. We also find this discouraging.

Why do you still have faith in this dangerous species? The massive comet will end human life on Earth, and nothing can stop that. For us to interfere would set loose a race of fanatics. The galaxy would be at risk if humans advanced exponentially and obtained quantum travel before controlling their destructive nature. Only civilizations that end their self-delusions and aggressions rise naturally to the next stage of survival.

Your request is denied.

Chapter 17

Quantum Tunneling

After months of research, dead ends, and rejections, James found a group of scientists with knowledge of quantum tunneling that agreed to meet with him.

"Did you say cosmic teleportation?" James asked.

"Yes, life on Earth is probably the result of our universe cheating," said Professor Marvin Adamson, lead theoretical physicist at Carnegie Mellon University. "Haven't you ever wondered how amino acids ended up on Earth?"

Fighting the urge to laugh, James feigned an interest. "Yes, that is a mystery, all right. Could you explain how that could result from quantum tunneling?"

"According to our research team, which included scientists from the Max Planck Institute and Friedrich Schiller University Jena, the origin of life on Earth probably began far out there in space.

Our team experimentally produced complex amino acids in a space-like environment. Previously, scientists believed life had to evolve on the Earth because of its proximity to the sun."

"But how did the amino acids form in space and then get from space to the Earth?" James asked.

"The universe cheated. You leave the laws of physics behind to overcome an impossible limit. The heart of the problem is that molecules have more thermal energy at higher temperatures. That is why combustion engines work.

"Let me explain. Out in cold space, molecules are lazy. They can't climb the energy barrier. So, our researchers relied on the universe's affinity for cheating to solve this. Instead of providing more energy, the universe teleports the molecules past the barrier and pretends like it never happened. And that is your crazy quantum process called 'tunneling.'"

"What?! Wait a minute. So the universe creates a tunnel through the energy barrier to let the molecules slip through?"

"Well, 'tunneling' is a bad word because it sounds like a particle is digging through a wall, but there is no hole or tunnel. A better term is 'probability,' quantum mechanics 'probability.' Think of amino acid molecules as an oscillating wave with the probability of being in a specific place. The wave cheats and continues inside the barrier and through to the other side at a smaller amplitude."

"All right. Once the amino acids magically appear in space, how do they reach Earth?" James asked.

"Part of these organics could be in the form of peptides. At later stages, this dust becomes the building blocks of comets and asteroids."

"Now you have my attention. In your opinion, is it possible to use the wacky tunneling for faster-than-light space travel?" James already knew the answer, but he had no idea how it worked.

"In my opinion, yes. The sun shines because enough random particles tunnel past their distinct energy barriers to cause the chemical reactions necessary to keep it burning. And that is a lot of power. Some on our team believe it might be possible to teleport an entire planet."

James fell silent for a spell before responding. "How could we test this? Have you ever thought about that?"

"Oh, sure. We just need a spaceship and some equipment humans have yet to invent," the professor chuckled.

"How fast can you gather your team? We need to get to Area 51!"

"I know you are kidding, but that's a good one. I need to get back to work, but it's been enjoyable meeting with you."

"Professor, I'm not kidding. Your spaceship and equipment are at Area 51. I'm about to tell you something that will shock you."

James signaled, and three soldiers and a strange-looking man with an oblong head approached. These men are from Area 51 and will help prepare your transportation."

"What is this?!" the Professor shouted and turned to leave.

James placed his hand on his shoulder, and the professor turned back angrily. "Marvin, the Earth is in peril. We leave next week."

Chapter 18

The Days of Wonder

"Why do you love Earth?" Juni asked. "Humans are a self-destructive species. They are at constant war with themselves. Their home planet is under continuous assault from their activities and selfishness."

James and Juni were on a trail above Alta, Utah, where Juni had agreed to meet with James following the alien rejection. "The days of wonder, Juni."

"The what? I do not understand."

"Juni, why do you speak so formally? It's okay to use colloquialisms. I don't mind," James said with a smile.

As Juni processed that comment, James found a lovely sunflower and placed it in her hair.

Juni seemed conflicted. "Don't touch me, James. It's forbidden."

James laughed. "Is that rule anything like the rule of non-interference? Is it worse for you to touch me or for you to save the Earth from a massive killer comet?"

"Both are forbidden, James," Juni replied. "Again, why do you love the Earth?"

"The days of wonder," James replied.

"What are the days of wonder?"

"From the summer of 1953 to the summer of 1964, America was in a gap between wars in Korea and Vietnam. Those were my years between five and sixteen. Life was simple and, well, fun. Those were the years of wonder and imagination, and the kids were crazy innocent.

"That was the Earth I learned to love. I know those innocent were kidnapped and sent to Vietnam, but it didn't have to be that way. Some stood up and said, 'Hell no, we won't go.' Remember Woodstock, Juni?

"I had terrific parents and sisters that teased me. Before getting my driver's license, I had a black lab that loved me and a Vespa scooter. The cops never caught me, and they tried. My dog rode on my scooter with me.

"But here's the thing, Juni: for me, the Earth was a place of wonder and imagination, not hatred and killing."

"But you lived in an isolated time and place, not typical of Earth in general. I understand, though, you see the potential. If your time was those days of wonder, then it is possible, unlikely but possible, that Earth could become a planet of wonder," Juni said without stopping as the sunflower fell from her hair.

"Exactly! Juni, Earth has the potential." James stooped and picked up the sunflower. As Juni turned to face him, James placed the flower back in her hair.

"You don't listen, James. There are timeless reasons for our rules. I will not punish you for the sunflower, but not interfering with the destiny of the Earth is something you must learn to accept."

"I told you, the cops could never catch me on my scooter. I suppose the punishment would have been harsh for a boy, but I sometimes thought they never wanted to catch me."

Juni moved closer, looking at James with mysterious, penetrating, almost frightening alien eyes. Moving even closer, she leaned forward and kissed him. "You have so much to do, James. You are the last hope for this wondrous Earth."

End of Book One...

Robert Adamson

Graduated from the University of Utah with a degree in Computer Science. Married with six adventurous children. I love the island of Kauai and science fiction, and mountain biking. My wife thinks I'm an Alien from another world.

I've been writing software since the golden age. I knew the founders of Novell, Microsoft, Borland, Evans & Sutherland, Pansophic, Apple (that's a fun story), Oracle, Electronic Data Systems, Computer Associates, and others. Most of the legends are gone now, but what a trip. They would dream about a world connected by computers.

Lately, I've been writing more Science Fiction. It's fun!

Other books by Robert Adamson

BASE: The Edge of Reality

The Old Mountain Biker

Hacking the Universe

www.robertgadamson.com

www.ingramcontent.com/pod-product-compliance
Lightning Source LLC
Chambersburg PA
CBHW010140030826
48979CB00023B/1047